PENGUIN BOOKS

GEMINI

Nikki Giovanni, one of America's most widely read living poets, entered the literary world at the height of the Black Arts Movement and quickly achieved not simple fame but stardom. A recording of her poems was one of the best-selling albums in the country; all but one of her nearly twenty books are still in print with several having sold more than a hundred thousand copies. Named woman of the year by three different magazines, including *Ebony*, and recipient of a host of honorary doctorates and awards, Nikki Giovanni has read from her work and lectured at colleges around the country. Her books include *Black Feeling, Black Talk/Black Judgement*; *My House*; *The Women and the Men*; *Cotton Candy on a Rainy Day*; *Those Who Ride the Night Winds*; and *Sacred Cows…and Other Edibles*. Nikki Giovanni is a professor of English at Virginia Polytechnic.

GEMINI

*An Extended Autobiographical
Statement on My First Twenty-Five
Years of Being a Black Poet*

Nikki Giovanni

Penguin Books

DEDICATION
To my son Thomas and Barb's son Anthony and their fathers, who
probably never thought they could produce anything as lovely as them.
NG

PENGUIN BOOKS
Published by the Penguin Group
Viking Penguin, a division of Penguin Books USA Inc.,
375 Hudson Street, New York, New York 10014, U.S.A.
Penguin Books Ltd, 27 Wrights Lane, London W8 5TZ, England
Penguin Books Australia Ltd, Ringwood, Victoria, Australia
Penguin Books Canada Ltd, 10 Alcorn Avenue, Suite 300,
Toronto, Ontario, Canada M4V 3B2
Penguin Books (N.Z.) Ltd, 182–190 Wairau Road, Auckland 10, New Zealand

Penguin Books Ltd, Registered Offices:
Harmondsworth, Middlesex, England

First published by The Bobbs-Merrill Company, Inc., 1971
Viking Compass Edition published 1973
Reprinted 1973 (twice), 1974 (twice), 1975
Published in Penguin Books 1976

11 13 15 14 12

ISBN 0 14 00.4264 4

Library of Congress catalog card number: 72-11674

This edition reprinted by arrangement with The Bobbs-Merrill Company, Inc.

Printed in the United States of America
Set in Linotype Caledonia

CONTENTS

Introduction, *by Barbara Crosby*   *vii*

1   *400 Mulvaney Street*   3

2   *For a Four-Year-Old*   13

3   *On Being Asked What It's Like to Be Black*   24

4   *A Revolutionary Tale*   34

5   *Don't Have a Baby till You Read This*   53

6   *It's a Case of . . .*   71

7   *A Spiritual View of Lena Horne*   86

8   *The Weather as a Cultural Determiner*   91

9   *The Beginning Is Zero*   100

10   *Black Poems,* Poseurs *and Power*   106

11   The Sound of Soul, *by Phyll Garland:*
A Book Review with a Poetic Insert   113

12   *Convalescence—Compared to What?*   122

13   *Gemini—a Prolonged Autobiographical Statement
on Why*   133

INTRODUCTION

---

by Barbara Crosby

Dear Anthony,

YOUR AUNT NIKKI is my best friend, Chris's favorite aunt, Tommy's
mommy and Louvenia's representative on earth. Maybe Louvenia
is one of the best explanations for all of the apparent contradictions
which ultimately always fit. Louvenia was one of the last strong
Black Southern ladies who would bash you over the head with an
umbrella if you didn't give M.L.K. proper respect. She was also
Nikki's grandmother.

If one believes that genes move toward perfection of character-
istics then Nikki, with the added props of being born a Gemini
seven, fell into an advanced stage of double realities, functioning
consistently within two seemingly contradictory realms simulta-
neously. Like she begs a nonpaying company to take a best-selling
work and refuses a company offering good advances. Or wears a
threadbare sweater ("But my sister made it for me") over an ex-
pensive velvet jumpsuit. Or develops a readership and following

among a group of people who have been traditionally considered nonreaders, and then has her writings rejected by slick, sophisticated magazines because they can't understand it. Could these be the regular conflicts of an Eastern nature living in a Western culture?

Being a Gemini only partially explains the difficulties inherent in the existence of this small, quick, harsh, gentle girl-woman. Another part is genius. Are geniuses known from birth or must they grow with their secret and maybe never even realize it themselves? The weird housewife or that scatterbrain sales clerk just might be nonfunctioning because of a million million thoughts which fall into emptiness. One must have a way of communicating, a way of organizing and sharing, for genius can be very lonely. Luckily Nikki realizes it, maybe through the results of white folks' tests or maybe because Louvenia told her, or maybe she just knew. At any rate she was left with the simpler task of figuring out how to use it.

When she was little she read Ayn Rand, cheap novels, books about the formation of clouds and fairy tales. She listened to Yolande and Gus, Flora and Theresa at the table and watched Gary's adventures into the big real world. She saw every B movie she could squeeze from her Sunday money after bus fare from the Valley to Cincinnati. Then she would secrete herself and write stories—only to hide them. One of a genius' earliest lessons is that her consciousness is considered bizarre by others so she hides away for fear of being misunderstood, and for fear.

As if she didn't have enough trouble already, poor Aunt Nikki was also blessed with a spiritual/emotional nature reaching back to her African roots. Dogs love her though she says that she is afraid of them. Cats have such a hold on her that she feels in direct conflict with them: she says they sit and stare and dare her to work. Her strongest affinity is to turtles, with which she has fantastic luck. They live for years unless she takes them out for air and loses them in the tall grass. Her idea of winter fun is a trip to the zoo with Chris, though I have never understood and neither did Louvenia why she hates parades.

She has a special ability and need to function with old ladies, and many of her girlfriends—from stars through social workers of various sizes—are over fifty. But her magic trick is communication with adolescents. I've sat in on her college classes and not understood a word she has said while all her students seemed to understand perfectly. Maybe I was listening with the wrong part. Maybe she was just communicating love to the Black soul and I was using Western-trained ears.

To me Nikki has been a friend. But the relationship has required energy and movement. Some great cracker once said that the greatest sin was being a bore. Nikki's personal growth has required that all around her grow. As she moves she pulls us all with her to new positions of intellectual and spiritual understanding. She is rejecting of weakness, which saps the strong. Ellis says that there are a few centripetal forces who draw others to them, artist-suns who form creative universes with the others as planets. Nikki is one of these.

Nikki is at this point in time a superstar in a remote area, a Black female poet with a television following that includes both the New York fly set and the Knoxville church ladies. She is pretty and eccentric—some would call her wild; this depends on your point of identification. She curses with a style and sense of the genteel, a freedom and control in an admirable balance that is impossible to imitate. Those who are attracted by her glamour and try to copy it find that the shoes pinch awfully. I would warrant there is only one human being who takes Nikki for granted: her son, Thomas, who came to give love and break up chairs, who came to say, "You are not alone."

So now, with the category of Black motherhood to add to her definition, she is sailing through adulthood like a flying fish jumping to bait or an egret heading for the elephants, touching all elements—land, water and air. The fire is within. The fire from which the phoenix emerges.

At this writing she is still growing, and I wouldn't presume to understand her. All I know is that she is the most cowardly, bravest, least understanding, most sensitive, slowest to anger, most quixotic, lyingest, most honest woman I know. To love her is to love contradictions and conflict. To know her is never to understand but to be sure that all is life.

And when I asked Nikki what *Gemini* was all about she said proudly and definitely, "A fictionalized autobiographical account of my first twenty-five years." I asked her, "What does that mean?" And she looked up from her desk with the kind of impatience she has with me to say, "Barbara, how would I know?"

GEMINI

Gary, my sister; Louvenia, my grandmother; Gus, my father, with me in his lap; Yolande, my mother; my aunt Gladys

1

400 Mulvaney Street

I was going to Knoxville, Tennessee, to speak. I was going other places first but mostly to me I was going home. And I, running late as usual, hurried to the airport just in time.

The runway is like an aircraft carrier—sticking out in the bay—and you always get the feeling of drunken fly-boys in green airplane hats chomping wads and wads of gum going "Whooooopie!" as they bring the 747 in from Hackensack to La Guardia. It had been snowing for two days in New York and the runway was frozen. They never say to you that the runway is frozen and therefore dangerous to take off from, and in fact you'd never notice it because all the New York airports have tremendous backups—even on clear days. So sitting there waiting was not unusual but I did notice this tendency to slide to the side with every strong wind, and I peeked out my window and noticed we were in the tracks of the previous jet and I thought: death has to eat too. And I went to sleep.

The whole thing about going to Knoxville appealed to my vanity. I had gotten a call from Harvey Glover about coming down and had said yes and had thought no more of it. Mostly, as you probably notice, artists very rarely have the chance to go back home and say, "I think I've done you proud." People are so insecure and in some cases jealous and in some cases think so little of themselves in general that they seldom think you'd be really honored to speak in your home town or at your old high school. And other people are sometimes so contemptuous of home that they in fact don't want to come back. This has set up a negative equation between the artist and home.

I was excited about going to Knoxville but I didn't want to get my hopes up. What if it fell through? What if they didn't like me? Oh, my God! What if nobody came to hear me? Maybe we'd better forget about it. And I did. I flew on out to Cleveland to make enough money to be able to go to Knoxville. And Cleveland was beautiful. A girl named Pat and her policeman friend couldn't have been any nicer. And he was an intelligent cop. I got the feeling I was going to have a good weekend. Then my mother met me at the Cincinnati airport, where I had to change over, and had coffee with me and had liked my last television appearance. Then they called my flight, and on to Knoxville.

WHEN WE WERE GROWING UP Knoxville didn't have television, let alone an airport. It finally got TV but the airport is in Alcoa. And is now called Tyson Field. Right? Small towns are funny. Knoxville even has a zip code and seven-digit phone numbers. All of which seems strange to me since I mostly remember Mrs. Flora Ford's white cake with white icing and Miss Delaney's blue furs and Armetine Picket's being the sharpest woman in town—she attended our church—and Miss Brooks wearing tight sweaters and Carter-Roberts Drug Store sending out Modern Jazz Quartet sounds of "Fontessa" and my introduction to Nina Simone by David Cherry, dropping a nickel in the jukebox and "Porgy" coming out. I mostly remember Vine Street, which I was not allowed to walk to get to school, though Grandmother didn't want me to take Paine Street either because Jay Manning lived on it and he was home from the army and very beautiful with his Black face and two dimples. Not that I was going to do anything, because I didn't do anything enough even to think in terms of not doing anything, but according to small-town logic "It looks bad."

The Gem Theatre was on the corner of Vine and a street that runs parallel to the creek, and for 10 cents you could sit all day and see a double feature, five cartoons and two serials plus previews for the next two weeks. And I remember Frankie Lennon would come in with her gang and sit behind me and I wanted to say, "Hi. Can I sit with you?" but thought they were too snooty, and they, I found out later, thought I was too Northern and stuck-up. All of that is gone now. Something called progress killed my grandmother.

Mulvaney Street looked like a camel's back with both humps bulging—up and down—and we lived in the down part. At the top of the left hill a lady made ice balls and would mix the flavors for you for just a nickel. Across the street from her was the Negro center, where the guys played indoor basketball and the little kids went for stories and nap time. Down in the valley part were the tennis courts, the creek, the bulk of the park and the beginning of the right hill. To enter or leave the street you went either up or down. I used to think of it as a fort, especially when it snowed, and the enemy would always try to sneak through the underbrush nurtured by the creek and through the park trees, but we always spotted strangers and dealt. As you came down the left hill the houses were up on its side; then people got regular flat front yards; then the right hill started and ran all the way into Vine and Mulvaney was gone and the big apartment building didn't have a yard at all.

Grandmother and Grandpapa had lived at 400 since they'd left

Georgia. And Mommy had been a baby there and Anto and Aunt Agnes were born there. And dated there and sat on the swing on the front porch and fussed there, and our good and our bad were recorded there. That little frame house duplicated twice more which overlooked the soft-voiced people passing by with "Evening, 'Fessor Watson, Miz Watson," and the grass wouldn't grow between our house and Edith and Clarence White's house. It was said that he had something to do with numbers. When the man tried to get between the two houses and the cinder crunched a warning to us, both houses lit up and the man was caught between Mr. White's shotgun and Grandfather's revolver, trying to explain he was lost. Grandpapa would never pull a gun unless he intended to shoot and would only shoot to kill. I think when he reached Knoxville he was just tired of running. I brought his gun to New York with me after he died but the forces that be don't want anyone to keep her history, even if it's just a clogged twenty-two that no one in her right mind would even load.

Mr. and Mrs. Ector's rounded the trio of houses off. He always wore a stocking cap till he got tied back and would emerge very dapper. He was in love with the various automobiles he owned and had been seen by Grandmother and me on more than one occasion sweeping the snow from in front of his garage before he would back the car into the street. All summer he parked his car at the bottom of the hill and polished it twice a day and delighted in it. Grandmother would call across the porches to him, "Ector, you a fool 'bout that car, ain't cha?" And he would smile back. "Yes, ma'am." We were always polite with the Ectors because they had neither children nor grandchildren so there were no grounds for familiarity. I never knew Nellie Ector very well at all. It was rumored that she was a divorcée who had latched on to him, and to me she became all the tragic heroines I had read about, like *Forever Amber* or the *All This and Heaven Too* chick, and I was awed but kept my distance. He was laughs, though. I don't know when it happened to the Ectors but Mr. White was the first to die.

I considered myself a hot-shot canasta player and I would play three-hand with Grandmother and Mrs. White and beat them. But I would drag the game on and on because it seemed so lonely next door when I could look through my bedroom window and see Mrs. White dressing for bed and not having to pull the shade anymore.

You always think the ones you love will always be there to love you. I went on to my grandfather's alma mater and got kicked out and would have disgraced the family but I had enough style for it not to be considered disgraceful. I could not/did not adjust to the Fisk social life and it could not/did not adjust to my intellect, so Thanksgiving I rushed home to Grandmother's without the bitchy dean of women's permission and that dean put me on social probation. Which would have worked but I was very much in love and not about to consider her punishment as anything real I should deal with. And the funny thing about that Thanksgiving was that I knew everything would go down just as it did. But I still wouldn't have changed it because Grandmother and Grandpapa would have had dinner alone and I would have had dinner alone and the next Thanksgiving we wouldn't even have him and Grandmother and I would both be alone by ourselves, and the only change would have been that Fisk considered me an ideal student, which means little on a life scale. My grandparents were surprised to see me in my brown slacks and beige sweater nervously chain-smoking and being so glad to touch base again. And she, who knew everything, never once asked me about school. And he was old so I lied to him. And I went to Mount Zion Baptist with them that Sunday and saw he was going to die. He just had to. And I didn't want that. Because I didn't know what to do about Louvenia, who had never been alone in her life.

I left Sunday night and saw the dean Monday morning. She asked where I had been. I said home. She asked if I had permission. I said I didn't need her permission to go home. She said, "Miss Giovanni," in a way I've been hearing all my life, in a way I've heard so long I know I'm on the right track when I hear it, and shook her head. I was "released from the school" February 1 because my "attitudes did not fit those of a Fisk woman." Grandpapa died in April and I was glad it was warm because he hated the cold so badly. Mommy and I drove to Knoxville to the funeral with Chris—Gary's, my sister's, son—and I was brave and didn't cry and made decisions. And finally the time came and Anto left and Aunt Agnes left. And Mommy and Chris and I stayed on till finally Mommy had to go back to work. And Grandmother never once asked me about Fisk. We got up early Saturday morning and Grandmother made fried chicken for us. Nobody said we were leaving but we were. And we all walked down the hill to the car. And kissed. And I looked at her standing there so bravely trying not to think what I was trying not to feel. And I got in on the driver's side and looked at her standing there with her plaid apron and her hair in a bun, her feet hanging loosely out of her mules, sixty-three years old, waving good-bye to us, and for the first time having to go into 400 Mulvaney without John Brown Watson. I felt like an impotent dog. If I couldn't protect this magnificent woman, my grandmother, from loneliness, what could I ever do? I have always hated death. It is unacceptable to kill the young and distasteful to watch the old expire. And those in between our link commit the little murders all the time. There must be a better way. So Knoxville decided to become a model city and a new mall was built to replace the old marketplace and they were talking about convention centers and expressways. And Mulvaney Street was a part of it all. This progress.

And I looked out from a drugged sleep and saw the Smoky Mountains looming ahead. The Smokies are so called because the clouds hang low. We used to camp in them. And the bears would come into camp but if you didn't feed them they would go away. It's still a fact. And we prepared for the landing and I closed my eyes as I always do because landings and takeoffs are the most vulnerable times for a plane, and if I'm going to die I don't have to watch it coming. It is very hard to give up your body completely. But the older I get the more dependent I am on other people for my safety, so I closed my eyes and placed myself in harmony with the plane.

Tyson Field turned out to be Alcoa. Progress again. And the Alcoa Highway had been widened because the new governor was a football fan and had gotten stuck on the old highway while trying to make a University of Tennessee football game and had missed the kickoff. The next day they began widening the road. We were going to the University of Tennessee for the first speaking of the day. I would have preferred Knoxville College, which had graduated three Watsons and two Watson progeny. It was too funny being at U.T. speaking of Blackness because I remember when Joe Mack and I integrated the theater here to see *L'il Abner*. And here an Afro Liberation Society was set up. Suddenly my body remembered we hadn't eaten in a couple of days and Harvey got me a quart of milk and the speaking went on. Then we left U.T. and headed for Black Knoxville.

Gay Street is to Knoxville what Fifth Avenue is to New York. Something special, yes? And it looked the same. But Vine Street, where I would sneak to the drugstore to buy *Screen Stories* and watch the men drink wine and play pool—all gone. A wide, clean military-looking highway has taken its place. Austin Homes is cordoned off. It looked like a big prison. The Gem Theatre is now some sort of nightclub and Mulvaney Street is gone. Completely wiped out. Assassinated along with the old people who made it live. I looked over and saw that the lady who used to cry "HOT FISH! GOOD HOT FISH!" no longer had a Cal Johnson Park to come to and set up her stove in. Grandmother would not say, "Edith White! I think I'll send Gary for a sandwich. You want one?" Mrs. Abrum and her reverend husband from rural Tennessee wouldn't bring us any more goose eggs from across the street. And Leroy wouldn't chase his mother's boyfriend on Saturday night down the back alley anymore. All gone, not even to a major highway but to a cutoff of a cutoff. All the old people who died from lack of adjustment died for a cutoff of a cutoff.

And I remember our finding Grandmother the house on Linden Avenue and constantly reminding her it was every bit as good as if not better than the little ole house. A bigger back yard and no steps to climb. But I knew what Grandmother knew, what we all knew. There was no familiar smell in that house. No coal ashes from the fireplaces. Nowhere that you could touch and say, "Yolande threw her doll against this wall," or "Agnes fell down these steps." No smell or taste of biscuits Grandpapa had eaten with the Alaga syrup he loved so much. No Sunday chicken. No sound of "Lord, you children don't care a thing 'bout me after all I done for you," because Grandmother always had the need to feel mistreated. No spot in the back hall weighted down with lodge books and no corner where the old record player sat playing Billy Eckstine crooning, "What's My Name?" till Grandmother said, "Lord! Any fool know his name!" No breeze on dreamy nights when Mommy would listen over and over again to "I Don't See Me in Your Eyes Anymore." No pain in my knuckles where Grandmother had rapped them because she was determined I would play the piano, and when that absolutely failed, no effort on Linden for us to learn the flowers. No echo of me being the only person in the history of the family to curse Grandmother out and no Grandpapa saying, "Oh, my," which was serious from him, "we can't have this." Linden Avenue was pretty but it had no life.

And I took Grandmother one summer to Lookout Mountain in Chattanooga and she would say I was the only grandchild who would take her riding. And that was the summer I noticed her left leg was shriveling. And she said I didn't have to hold her hand and I said I liked to. And I made ice cream the way Grandpapa used to do almost every Sunday. And I churned butter in the hand churner. And I knew and she knew that there was nothing I could do. "I just want to see you graduate," she said, and I didn't know she meant it. I graduated February 4. She died March 8.

And I went to Knoxville looking for Frankie and the Gem and Carter-Roberts or something and they were all gone. And 400 Mulvaney Street, like a majestic king dethroned, put naked in the streets to beg, stood there just a mere skeleton of itself. The cellar that had been so mysterious was now exposed. The fireplaces stood. And I saw the kitchen light hanging and the peach butter put up on the back porch and I wondered why they were still there. She was dead. And I heard the daily soap operas from the radio we had given her one birthday and saw the string beans cooking in the deep well and thought how odd, since there was no stove, and I wanted to ask how Babbi was doing since I hadn't heard or seen "Brighter Day" in so long but no one would show himself. The roses in the front yard were blooming and it seemed a disgrace. Probably the tomatoes came up that year. She always had fantastic luck with tomatoes. But I was just too tired to walk up the front steps to see. Edith White had died. Mr. Ector had died, I heard. Grandmother had died. The park was not yet gone but the trees looked naked and scared. The wind sang to them but they wouldn't smile. The playground where I had swung. The courts where I played my first game of tennis. The creek where our balls were lost. "HOT FISH! GOOD HOT FISH!" The hill where the car speeding down almost hit me. Walking barefoot up the hill to the center to hear stories and my feet burning. All gone. Because progress is so necessary. General Electric says, "Our most important product." And I thought Ronald Reagan was cute.

I was sick throughout the funeral. I left Cincinnati driving Mommy, Gary and Chris to Knoxville. From the moment my father had called my apartment I had been sick because I knew before they told me that she was dead. And she had promised to visit me on the tenth. Chris and I were going to drive down to get her since she didn't feel she could fly. And here it was the eighth. I had a letter from her at my house when I got back reaffirming our plans for her visit. I had a cold. And I ran the heat the entire trip despite the sun coming directly down on us. I couldn't get warm.

And we stopped in Kentucky for country ham and I remembered how she used to hoard it from us and I couldn't eat. And I drove on. Gary was supposed to relieve me but she was crying too much. And the car was too hot and it was all so unnecessary. She died because she didn't know where she was and didn't like it. And there was no one there to give a touch or smell or feel and I think I should have been there. And at her funeral they said, "It is well," and I knew she knew it was. And it was so peaceful in Mount Zion Baptist Church that afternoon. And I hope when I die that it can be said of me all is well with my soul.

So they took me up what would have been Vine Street past what would have been Mulvaney and I thought there may be a reason we lack a collective historical memory. And I was taken out to the beautiful homes on Brooks Road where we considered the folks "so swell, don't cha know." And I was exhausted but feeling quite high from being once again in a place where no matter what I belong. And Knoxville belongs to me. I was born there in Old Knoxville General and I am buried there with Louvenia. And as the time neared for me to speak I had no idea where I would start. I was nervous and afraid because I just wanted to quote Gwen Brooks and say, "This is the urgency—Live!" And they gave me a standing ovation and I wanted to say, "Thank you," but that was hardly sufficient. Mommy's old bridge club, Les Pas Si Bêtes, gave me beads, and that's the kind of thing that happens in small towns where people aren't afraid to be warm. And I looked out and saw Miss Delaney in her blue furs. And was reminded life continues. And I saw the young brothers and sisters who never even knew me or my family and I saw my grandmother's friends who shouldn't even have been out that late at night. And they had come to say *Welcome Home*. And I thought Tommy, my son, must know about this. He must know we come from somewhere. That we belong.

2

For a Four-Year-Old

FOR A FOUR-YEAR-OLD I was a terror. Mostly this was because my big sister, Gary, would wolf all the time, then come running in from school, throw her books down and scream at my mother, "JUST LET ME GO GET THEM—JUST LET ME AT THEM!" And Mommy, digging the whole scene, would say, "Gary, have a glass of milk and some graham crackers and let's talk about your day." And Gary would say, "But Peggy's waiting outside. I gotta go fight." And I, sitting on the top porch waiting for Gary to come home, would already have adequately handled the situation. Since it was a thrice-weekly occurrence at least, I kept a large supply of large rocks on the top porch. And as Gary crossed the front porch I had started pelting Peggy and her gang with my pieces. So by the time Gary put her books down and called out how she had to fight, I had them on the run. For a four-year-old I was beautiful. Peggy and her gang would always run out of my reach and call up, "YOU TELL GARY WE'LL GET HER! YOU AIN'T ALWAYS HOME!" Then they'd leave.

By the time Gary had changed clothes and had her first glass of milk it was all over. Mommy innocently asked where I had been, telling me, "Gary's home." And I said, "Yeah, Peggy chased her again. But I took care of it." "Kim, you've got to quit fighting so much. You'll be five soon and in school yourself. And you've got to control yourself."

"I'm glad Kim got that ole Miss Yella," Gary piped up from her plate. "She's always picking on somebody." "Somebody's always wolfing," Mommy said. "And who are you to call anybody yellow?" "Well, at least my hair don't hang all the way down to the ground." "Doesn't. Doesn't hang. And Kim, you'll have to quit storing those rocks on the porch. Gary can fight her own battles." "Yes, Mommy."

The summer passed rather happily with Peggy and sometimes Skippy chasing Gary from piano lessons. I always thought Gary was tops. She is very smooth, with the older sister style that says I-can-do-anything, you know? And I thought she could. "Kim," she said, taking me aside in the back yard, "you know why I don't fight? It's not that I'm scared or something—but I'm a musician. What if my hands were maimed? What if I were injured or something? Then Dr. Matthews couldn't give me lessons anymore. Then Mrs. Clarke couldn't give me rehearsals anymore. Why, their families would starve. Walter and Charles couldn't wear clothes. The studio would close down. And the world would be deprived of a great talent playing 'Claire de Lune.' You understand, don't you?" And I did. I swear I did. All I wanted from this world was to protect and nourish this great talent, who was not my cousin or best friend or next-door neighbor but my very own sister.

I had turned five at the end of the school year and would be going to school myself in the fall. I had a mission in life. No one must touch Gary. "Kim," Mommy said, "you know Gary says a lot of things that are true but not as true as she makes them sound." And I thought no one, not even our mother, appreciated the mission Gary and I had. She must be free to work. Really! If I hadn't been prepared to deal I don't think Gary would have survived—with her frivolous music and fancy ideas. That's the stuff extinction is made of. In my own little anti-intellectual way I understood a profundity. It is un-American, if not dangerous, not to fight. I felt I stood alone.

We lived in Wyoming, Ohio, which is a suburb of Cincinnati, which some say is a suburb of Lexington, Kentucky. But we liked it. The sidewalks run broad and clear; the grass and mud intertwine just enough to let you be a muddy little lady; and there were those magnificent little violets that some called weeds and that I would pick for Mommy to put in her window vase.

Most of the summer was spent running and swinging and making believe. I did learn the hard way not to make-believe and swing at the same time. I was going way up high. People were standing at the bottom marveling at me. "She doesn't spell or read as well as Gary," they said, "but clearly she's an Olympic contender at swinging." They were amazed. Then I fell out of the swing. I wasn't so hurt as I was hurt. Swinging was my strong point. It's really a cruel life when your strong point falls through. But I had a backup. Gary had taught me how to read and write a little and I could count to ten in French, Okinawan and Pig Latin. I knew no matter what, I was going to knock kindergarten out. When fall finally came I was overprepared. I had even practiced nap time.

I woke up that morning bright and early to a solid cold cereal breakfast. You see, I had early recognized the importance of getting away from the hot-cereal-Father-John's-Tonic syndrome. The older you are the less they—i.e., parents—care what you eat until you get married or something. Then they—i.e., lovers—start the whole parent syndrome all over again. So I had told Mommy in no uncertain terms—*cold cereal, no toast, no Father John's and plenty of coffee.* She at least let me have the corn flakes.

She also insisted on taking me to school. Surely that was an insidious move on her part. I had planned to walk with Gary and let everybody know that just because I was going to school I wasn't going to be no lady or nothing like that. What I had done to Peggy last year I could do again.

You see, the winter before, Mommy had let me go meet Gary from school. That had been right after Christmas. Gary had taken the sled to school because we had finally gotten snow in January. I was going to meet her and ride home. Mommy had bundled me in my brown snowsuit and airplane hat pulled over my ears and mittens (though I had been insisting on gloves for some time) and a big scarf. Mommy took her job of mommying quite seriously and never wanted me to catch cold or something. I practically rolled down the stair and, gaining momentum, bounced along Burns Street, making the turn at Pendry past Mrs. Spears's house, just barely turning Oak and managing by the grace of God to stop in front of Oak Avenue school. Gary alighted from the side door with the sled and Peggy on her heels. We put her books on the beautiful beige sled with the magnificent red streak and started home, Peggy and the three goony girls a respectful distance behind.

"What will we do if they bother us?" Gary asked. "I'll beat her up." "Well, it's different when we're home but we've got the sled to look out for." "Don't worry, Gary, I'll beat her up." "Well, she better not hurt you or I'll deal with her myself." "Oh, no, Gary. Don't you get in it. I can beat Peggy all by myself." Even then I couldn't bear the thought of someone's laying uncaring, irreverent hands on her. "I can handle it." We turned the corner.

Pendry is one of those little suburb streets that they always show when they want to convince you Negroes want to live next door. The sidewalks are embraced by cut grass in the summer and a clean blanket of snow in the winter. All the houses have front yards and white steps leading to them. Mostly they are brick houses, except the Spearses had a white frame one. As we turned onto Pendry the gang moved up on us since no one from the school could see. "Look at the stuck-up boobsie twins," they started. "Mama had to send the baby to look out for the coward."

"Don't say anything," I advised. "You always say something to make them mad. Maybe they'll just leave us alone." We made it past the house where we never saw the people and started by Dr. Richardson's. "They walk alike, talk alike and roll on their bellies like a reptile," they chanted. There had been a circus that year and everybody had gotten into the barker thing. "Just look at them, folks. One can't do without the other." And they burst out laughing. "Hey, old stuck-up. What you gonna do when your sister's tired of fighting for you?" "I'll beat you up myself. That's what." Damn, damn, damn. Now we would have to fight. "You and what army, 'ho'?" *'Ho'* was always a favorite. "Me and yo' mama's army," Gary answered with precision and dignity. "You talking 'bout my mama?" "I would but the whole town is so I can't add nothing." They sidled up alongside us at the Spears's. "You take it back, Gary." Deadly quiet. "Yo' mama's so ugly she went to the zoo and the gorilla paid to see her." "You take that back!" "Yo' mama's such a 'ho' she went to visit a farm and they dug a whole field before they knew it was her."

Peggy swung and I stepped in. Peggy had long brown hair that she could easily have sat on if she wasn't always careful to fling it out of the way. She said it was her Indian ancestry. She swung her whole body to hit Gary as her goony girls formed a circle to watch. And as she swung I grabbed her hair, and began to wrap it around my hand, then my arm. I had a good, solid grip. Gary stepped back to watch the action. Mrs. Spears went to call Mommy. The next clear thing I remember is Mommy saying from a long, long way away, "Let her go, Kim," and Peggy being under me and me wondering why it was so cold. I, at four, had defeated Peggy Johnson. And she was bad. As Mommy fussed me home that was all I could think about. I had won. Now that that was established the rest would be simple.

So Mommy walked me to school telling me how nice the kids were and how I would enjoy it and I was thinking whether Peggy would remember last year and how I could make sure she knew the same would hold true. She must not, no one must touch my sister. "You must realize Gary is in the fifth grade and can fight for herself. You'll have enough to do just taking care of yourself. Your sister isn't a dummy. She skipped, didn't she? And she's not a weakling. She beats you up when you have arguments and I don't want any repetition of what happened last year. OK?" "Yes, Mommy." "I'm counting on you, Kim. It's very important you give the children a chance. You can't always run around with Gary and her friends. Make some of your own. If you give them a chance they'll just love you as much as your father and I do. OK?" "Yes, Mommy."

"Mrs. Hicks is a wonderful woman." "I remember Aunt Willa, Mommy. I like her and Elizabeth Ann." Sometimes I played with Elizabeth Ann even though she was younger than I. Aunt Willa was super. She played Pekeno at our house and sometimes they let me deal since I was always up and meddling. Aunt Willa would always pay you when you gave her a good hand. Some of Mommy's friends would just say, "Good dealing," and some would say, "Kim, why aren't you in bed?" But Aunt Willa was all right. She was always straight. You could really go to kindergarten with a lady like that. "And remember everybody in class doesn't know her like you do. So what are we going to call her?" "Mrs. Hicks," I pronounced very distinctly, "just like you said I should." "That's my big girl." Mommy squeezed my hand and looked relieved. Adults are certainly strange. They always do things they don't want people to remember but they never remember not to let you see them doing it. I mean, if they cared in the first place, it would have gone down differently. But what the hell—I would call Aunt Willa Mrs. Hicks and be good because I dug the whole game. Even then. From a low vantage point.

I was bouncing up the stairs prepared to knock them dead when Mommy opened the door and I looked at all those little faces. I broke down. I didn't know these people. They didn't look like they were seeing a woman with a mission. My God!! They might not even care. I started crying. Mommy, in the usual vanity that mothers possess, thought I didn't want to leave her but that wasn't it at all. I was entering a world where few knew and even fewer would ever understand my mission. Life is a motherfucker. Mommy—four eleven, ninety pounds after Christmas dinner—walked out of that kindergarten room a little taller, a bit prouder . . . her baby girl really cared. The kids, in their usual indifferent way, stated, "Kim is a crybaby." I wanted to shout at them all—*"You dumbbumbs"*—but I restrained myself by burying my head in Aunt Willa's lap and softly pleading, "What shall I do?" Aunt Willa hit upon the saving idea: Go get Gary.

In She strode—like Cleopatra on her barge down the Nile, like Nefertiti on her way to sit for the statue, like Harriet Tubman before her train or Mary Bethune with Elenora; my big sister came to handle the situation. You could feel the room respond to her presence. It could have been San Francisco at the earthquake, Chicago as Mrs. O'Leary walked to her cow, Rome as Nero struck up his fiddle, Harlem when Malcolm mounted the podium; Gary came to handle the situation. Looking neither right nor left she glided from the door, her eyes searching for the little figure buried in Aunt Willa's skirt. "Kim"—her voice containing all the power of Cicero at the seashore, Elijah at the annual meeting—"Kim, don't cry." And it was over. Tears falling literally pulled themselves back into my eyes. In a gulp, with a wipe of the hand, it was over. "I'll walk you home for lunch. Come on, now, and play with the other kids. There's Donny, Robert's brother, and Pearl. They want to play with you." The pain, the absolute pain of wanting to be eight years old and in the fifth grade and sophisticated and in control. I could have burst! "I'm sorry." "Don't worry about it. Mommy just wouldn't want you to cry." She turned her full gaze on me. "I've got to go back to class now." She paused. Of course I understood. Oh, yes. I understood. "See you at lunch," she whispered. And as majestically as she had come—red turtleneck sweater, white short socks and yes, sneakers (I still had to wear high-top shoes)—she vanished through the door. And I had been chosen to nourish this great woman, to protect her and perhaps, should I prove worthy, guide her.

For some reason, probably a blood thing, I was always good with my hands . . . and feet . . . and teeth . . . and I had a very good eye. If this wasn't the age of Black Power I would possibly attribute that to my Indian blood, but now I'm sure it goes straight to my Watusi grandfather and Amazon great-grandaunt. Skippy, an old enemy who I later learned planned to marry Gary, was pulling her hair and marking her knees up with his ballpoint. Gary would tell me of these things laughingly and I would exclaim, *"It's so wrong of him to abuse you,"* not to mention, in such a white way, "I will take care of it." She assured me, "It's all right, Kim. He's just teasing." But mine was not a world of frivolity. He was disturbing the genius. He was, in fact, not just disrespectful, because that at least means you understand the position; was not in reality just insolent, because that just means you are jealous—he was common! I had no choice. I called him out.

I would imagine no boy likes to be called out by a kindergartner, especially on the playground . . . especially to a marble duel. Plus he recognized what I didn't—he was in a trick. If he defeated me, he was supposed to. If he lost—my God! A nine-year-old boy losing? To me? My God! In deadly calm I drew the circle.

Now, our family was never what anyone could call well off. Mommy didn't work, but that was because the money would have been spent in babysitting fees. Gus, our father, held down a couple of jobs, which meant we rarely saw him. Grandmother had never actually worked either, but we're from a small town and Grandpapa was a schoolteacher—of Latin actually—which says a lot about our pretensions. But despite hard times, depressions, lack of real estate, we had passed, from generation to generation since we had first been brought to these shores, a particular semiprecious jewel that was once oblong in shape. It was originally brown with a green tint. In order to conceal it successfully through several hundred years of slavery we had worn it in odd places. It had been rounded off through the sweat and kisses of generations of Giovanni-Watson ancestors. We consulted it for every important and quite a few unimportant events and decisions.

When I decided to challenge Skippy I snuck the jewel from my mother's hiding place. As I drew the circle and stood back I was all confidence. There was no chance for the poor fellow. "You go first," I generously offered with the assurance of Willy McCovey at third base nodding to the pitcher to play ball. A sure winner. "No, you go first." Quietly, with a Huey Newton kind of rage. "You can go on." Smiling, prancing like Assault at the Derby. "You go on, Kim. You should get at least one chance." "One chance!" I knelt and spotted. There was no stopping me. I shot marbles from between my legs and over my back. I put a terrible double spin on my shot that knocked his cat's-eye out and came back for his steelie. I was baaaaad. I shot from under my arm and once while yawning. Good God! There was no way to defeat me! I rose from the earth brushing off the little specks that clung to my dress, tip chest two miles out. "And if you mess with my sister again I'll deal with you on a physical level." I was ready for anything. He squared off. "You keep it up, Kim, and somebody's gonna really get you." I half stepped back. "You, Mighty Mouse? You?" Sure, all the kids knew I could handle myself but teachers never know anything. I had him in a double bind. All the grown-ups ever saw was big brown eyes, three pigtails and high-top white shoes. He would really catch it if they saw him fighting—me especially. My stock in trade was that I looked so innocent. So he backed down. I understand his problem now, but then—a chicken at the top of the pecking heap—I ruled the roost. And as I sauntered happily up Oak Avenue, turned on Pendry, passed the Spears's house and headed for Burns Avenue I was feeling *très* good. Plus Mommy gave me my very favorite cold lunch—liverwurst with mayonnaise dripping from the raisin bread. Too much! I was prepared to take a long nap. I was prepared to work the number problems Gus had left for me. I was ready for everything . . . but Gary's reaction at 3:30.

"HOW COULD YOU DO THAT TO HIM?" "Who?" "HOW COULD YOU? MOMMY, KIM'SPICKINGONMYFRIENDS!" "Who, Gary?" My God! Her absolute displeasure. No "Hi." No "How'd it go today?" No approving smile. "Who, Gary?" "MOMMY, SHE MADE SKIPPY LOOK LIKE A FOOL!" "Skippy?" "YOU SHOULD HAVE SEEN HER!" "But he was picking on you." "I AM MORTIFIED!" "Mortified?"

My world was coming to an end. And all because of Skippy. I would handle this right away.

I ran out of the house like a pig runs when a Muslim comes, near rage. Absolute rage. "SKIPPYYY!" All the way down to his house. With just a brief stop for some sort of weapon. I don't actually remember picking up that piece of cement but it was there —along with my trusty broomstick that Flappy had made for me. I flew down to the corner, though of course being careful to stay on my side of the street. "SKIPPYYY! COME OUT! I WANT TO FIGHT YOU!" And there he was. Buck teeth, pants hanging off, sneakers and all. "COME ON OUT." He was ready. I could see he had been building his supply of rocks. He threw. But missed. I ducked and started running back and forth. "COME ON OVER." "YOU KNOW I CAN'T CROSS THE STREET." My father and Skippy's father had made an agreement that I couldn't cross the street since I fought and beat Skippy a lot. But he was in a rage. "TRY TO MAKE ME LOOK LIKE A FOOL, OLE SILLY GIRL. I'LL GET YOU." "COME ON OVER." I was a streak of energy. I was the fire after the A bomb fell. All heat and light. "COME ON OVER." And he did. I wanted to devour him. To kill him slowly. To punish him beyond words able to describe the emotion. He looked both ways and was on my territory. Like the Black panther I leaped. And he feinted and landed a solid blow. I never felt it. I clawed at his face and pulled his shirt loose.

"*YoutoremyshirtI'llkillyou!*" And he bit me. We fell onto the lawn and people were all around. We squared off and I heard Mommy say, "I hope he gets her." It crushed my will. I had been prepared to draw blood. Gary was mad and Mommy was rooting for the opposition. He swung and landed flat on my nose. Blood spurted, as blood is wont to do. I didn't cry or even really feel hurt. I just looked at him, then picked up my broomstick and set off for home. People started consoling Mommy but she was just saying, "I'm glad. Maybe Kim'll learn she can't fight Gary's battles." And I was crushed. I walked from Mrs. Williams' house to mine without family, friends or loved ones. No one understood what I had tried to do. No one. I thought of *Beautiful Joe* and *Mistress Margaret, Heidi* and the *King of the Golden River*. And conceived of myself in that league. I think I smiled as I opened the door.

3

*On Being Asked
What It's Like to Be Black**

I'VE ALWAYS KNOWN I was colored. When I was a Negro I knew I was colored; now that I'm Black I know which color it is. Any identity crisis I may have had never centered on race. I love those long, involved, big-worded essays on "How I Discovered My Blackness" in twenty-five words or less which generally appear in some mass magazine—always somehow smelling like Coke or Kellogg's corn flakes—the prize for the best essay being a brass knuckle up your head or behind, if you make any distinction between the two.

It's great when you near your quarter-century mark and someone says, "I want an experience on how you came to grips with being colored." The most logical answer is, "I came to grips with Blackdom when I grabbed my mama"—but I'm told on "Julia" that we don't necessarily know our mothers are colored, and you

* Reprinted from *US*, New York, Bantam Books, October, 1969, pp. 94–101.

can win a great big medal if you say it loud. If your parents are colored we have found—statistically—the chances are quite high that so are you. If your parents are mixed the chances are even higher that you'll grow up to be a Nigger. And with the racial situation reaching the proportions that it has, the only people (consistent with history) able to discover anything at all are still honkies. Or if you haven't gotten it together by the time you go to preschool, then you're gonna be left out. Now, that's only on the subconscious level.

My father was a real hip down-home big-time dude from Cincinnati who, through a screw-a-YWCA-lady or kiss-a-nun program, was picked up from the wilds of the West End (pronounced deprived area), where he was wreaking havoc on the girls, and sent to college, mostly I imagine because they recognized him as being so talented. Or if not necessarily talented, then able to communicate well with people. He was sent to Knoxville College in Tennessee. Nestled lovingly in the bosom of the Great Smoky Mountains in the land of Davy Crockett and other heroes of Western civilization is Knoxville, Tennessee. Knoxville, in those times, was noted for *Thunder Road* starring Robert Mitchum and/or Polly Bergen of Helen Morgan fame; but when my father boarded the train to carry him back to his spiritual roots (it was just like my great-grandfather to be the only damned slave in northeastern Tennessee) all he saw were crackers—friendly crackers, mean crackers, liberal crackers, conservative crackers, dumb crackers, smart crackers and just all kinds of crackers, some of whom, much to his surprise, were Black crackers. He hit the campus, "the Nigger the world awaited," shiny head (because Afros were not in vogue), snappy dresser with the one suit he had and a big friendly smile to show them all that just because he was in the South he wasn't going to do like a lot of people and cry all the time and embarrass the school. In walks the fox.

Swishing her behind, most likely carrying a tennis racket and flinging her hair (which at that time hung down to what was

swishing) was the woman of the world, the prize of all times—
Mommy. Mommy has an illustrious background. Her family, the
Mighty Watsons, had moved to Knoxville because my grandmother was going to be lynched. Well, the family never actually
said she was going to get lynched. They always stressed the fact
that traveling late at night under a blanket in a buggy is fun, and
even more fun if a decoy sitting in a buggy is sent off in another
direction with Uncle Joe and Uncle Frank carrying guns. They
told us the guns were to salute good-bye to Louvenia, my grandmother, and John Brown ("Book") Watson, my grandfather.

If I haven't digressed too much already I want to say something
about Grandpapa. He was an extremely handsome man. Grandmother got the hots for him and like any shooting star just fell and
hit *splash*. Now, we in the family have always considered it unfortunate that Grandfather was married to another woman at that
time. And Grandmother, to make matters even more urgent, would
not give him none. Grandfather considered that more unfortunate
than his marriage. And since he was the intellectual of the family,
hence "Book," he assessed the situation and reached the logical
conclusion that he should marry my Grandmother.

The Watsons were quite pleased with Louvenia Terrell because
she was so cute and intelligent, but what they didn't know and
later learned to their chagrin was that she was terribly intolerant
when it came to white people. The Watson clan was the epitome of
"Let's get along with the whites"; Grandmother was the height of
"We ain't taking no shit, John Brown, off nobody." So the trouble
began.

First some white woman wanted to buy some flowers from
Grandmother's yard, and as Grandmother told it they were not for
sale. She didn't make her living growing flowers for white people.
The woman's family came back later to settle it. "John, yo' wife insulted ma wife and we gotta settle this thang." Grandpapa was perfectly willing to make accommodations but when the only satis-
factory action was Grandmother's taking twenty-five buggy-whip
lashes, he had to draw the line. "Mr. Jenkins, we've known each

other a long time. Our families have done business together. But this is too much." "John, we've gotta settle this thang." And about that time Uncle Joe, who always liked to hunt, came out of Grandpapa's house with his gun and powder and asked if he could be of any help. The Jenkinses left. The Watsons stayed up all night with a gun peeking from every window. The guns in those days were not repeaters so the youngsters in the family had been given complete instructions on how to clean and load in the shortest time possible. I'm told by my granduncles there was a general air of disappointment when nobody showed. After almost a week of keeping watch things reverted to normal. Grandpapa says the white dude told him later they didn't need the flowers anyway.

Then one Sunday afternoon Grandmother and Grandpapa were out strolling when a Jewish merchant asked them to come look at his material. He owned one of those old stores with bolts and bolts of material because most clothes were made, not store-bought. Well, they looked and looked. Grandmother had him pull bolts from way up high to way down low. Then she got bored and told Grandpapa she was ready to go.

Merchant: You mean you're not going to buy anything?

Grandmother [innocently]: No.

Merchant: You mean you had me pull all this material out and you're not going to buy anything?

Grandmother [a little tired]: My husband and I were walking down the street minding our own business when you asked us to come in. We did not ask you.

Grandfather [wary of the escalation in the exchange]: Let's go, Louvenia.

Grandmother [as she generally did when she was in an argument]: Hell, it's his own fault. [To the merchant] Nah, we don't want none of your material.

Grandfather [pinching and kicking at her]: Let's go, Louvenia.

Merchant [in the background screaming obscenities]: I'll have you horsewhipped for talking to me this way.

Grandmother [really wolfing now]: You and which cavalry troop? My husband will kill you if you come near me!

Grandfather [almost in tears]: Let's go, Louvenia.

They hurried to spread the alarm of impending danger. A woman in the next county had recently been lynched and her womb split open so there was no doubt in Grandfather's mind that the whites might follow through this time. A family meeting was called and all agreed that Grandmother and Grandfather (most especially Grandmother) had to leave Albany, Georgia. The sooner the better. When night came they climbed into a buggy, pulled a blanket over themselves and slept until they reached the Tennessee border. Having no faith in southern Tennessee they began again by public transportation to head North. The intention was to go to Washington, D. C., or Philadelphia, but when they found themselves still in Tennessee they agreed to settle at the first reasonable-sized town they came to—Knoxville. Grandfather settled Grandmother in a good church home and went back to Albany, where he taught school, to finish the term out. Grandfather was like that.

Three lovely daughters were born in four happy years. Grandmother settled down to play house. The girls were all right with Grandpapa but, as Grandmother always said, "John Brown always had plenty of toys," so naturally she had more fun than he did. The oldest child was my mother.

Now, Mommy was an intellectual, aristocratic woman, which in her time was not at all fashionable. She read, liked paintings, played tennis and liked to party a great deal. Had she been rich she would have followed the sun—going places, learning things and being just generally unable to hold a job and be useful. But Mommy made just one bad mistake in the scheme of things—she sashayed across the Knoxville College campus, hair swinging down to her behind, most probably carrying a tennis racket, and ran into a shiny-head Negro with a pretty suit on. He, being warm and friendly and definitely looking for a city girl to roost with, introduced himself. I have always thought that if his name hadn't been exotic she would never have given him a second thought; but Grandfather, whom my mother was so much like, had a weakness for Romance languages and here comes this smiling dude with Giovanni for a name. Mommy decided to take him home.

From the resulting union two girls were born: typical of me, I was the second. Gary, my sister, is what is commonly known to white people as a smart Nigger. In the correct tradition of we-don't-take-no-shit-off-nobody, she could wolf away for hours. I'm still amazed she hasn't risen to national fame for her sheer ability to rap. Me—I'm different. I generally don't like to get into arguments, but I did like to fight. Many's the night if I hadn't remembered my Grandfather's patrician blood I'd have been swinging a blade on the street—that is, until I became a Black and decided Black people should not fight each other under any circumstances. Gary would go out and blow off about what was going to happen if she didn't get what she wanted and, not getting it, would come in and tell me, "You've got to go fight Thelma [or Barbara or Flora] 'cause she's been messing with me." Folks in my home town still have a lot of respect for me dating back to those days.

How and why I became a fighter is still a mystery to me. If you believe in innateness, then I guess the only logical conclusion is that it's in my blood. But most of us have a history of fighting unless you are Whitney Young's daughter or Roy Wilkins's mother. And I'll even bet Roy's mother was a real scrapper. Through a series of discussions I was having with a social worker, I discovered I am not objective. Any feeling I may have for someone or something is based on how he or it relates to me. Like I don't go for people because they are rich or famous or everybody thinks they are so hip. I don't support institutions because they are successful, democratic and said to be the best in the world. If something is good to me I like it; if it hurts me I don't. This feeling is extended to my friends.

If someone or something abuses my friends then it has in effect hurt me, and I don't go for that even if *The New York Times* says it is the hippest thing going. Like I wasn't impressed with James Earl Jones as an actor because though he may have done a beautiful job as Jack Johnson, the role is an insult. I'm not impressed with America. It acts well, too. There are no objective standards when it comes to your life; this is crucial. Objective standards and objective feelings always lead to objectionable situations. I'm a revolutionary poet in a prerevolutionary world.

And dealing with Blackness as a cultural entity can only lead to revolution. America, as Rap Brown pointed out, has always moved militarily because it has no superior culture. We, as beginning revolutionists, ought to understand that. Great cultures have always fallen to great guns. They always will. That's not a subjective thought; it's a fact. Facts are only tools to gain control over yourself and other people. So white folks develop facts about us; we are developing facts about them. In the end it's always a power struggle.

I've been taught all my life that power is an absolute good, not because I'm objectively more fit to wield power but because subjectively if I don't wield it it will be wielded over me. Trade white racism for Black racism? Anytime, since I'm Black. But facts show that Black people by the definition of racism cannot be racist. Racism is the subjugation of one people by another because of their race, and everything I do to white people will be based on what they did to me. Even their Bible, the Christian one, says, "Do unto others as they have done unto you." And Black Christians are becoming more aware of the meaning behind the Golden Rule. It's only logical.

I believe in logic. Logic is not an exercise to prove "A implies B" but a spiritual understanding of the subjective situation and the physical movement necessary to place life in its natural order. Black people are the natural, hence logical, rulers of the world.

This is a fact. And it's illogical for me to assume any other stance or to allow any other possibility. It's self-negating. If you don't love your mama and papa then you don't love yourself. Fathers are very important people.

Black people have been slaves in America and the world. Some slaves cleaned, some cooked, some picked cotton, some oversaw the others, some killed slavemasters, some fucked the slavemaster (and his mama) at their demand. A slave has no control over whom he fucks. Check it. But that's not your father because some beast raped your mother. Neither is it your mother because some beast sneaked down to Uncle Tom's cabin. White folks with degrees in sociology like to make generic judgments about political situations. If your father was drafted and killed in World War I, World War II, the Korean conflict, or the Vietnam advisoryship, they don't tell you he deserted your mother (which he logically did if he went off to fight the enemy's wars). They tell you what a good dude he was and "Ain't you proud of that shiny new medal?" And you are proud of him and say, "My father was a great man," even though he was never around to be anything to you. If the same man had been run out of town or was not allowed to hold a job, or your mother couldn't get relief with him in the household, then you should look upon his leaving home with the same loyalty as if he had gone to fight a war (which he really did). Or look at them both with the same disdain. Neither was there to love you and your mother when you needed to be loved and protected. One of the jobs of a father it to protect and provide, as best he can, for his family. This is related to power.

All Black men in the world today are out of power. Power only means the ability to have control over your life. If you don't have control you cannot take responsibility. That's what makes that latter-generation Irishman's report on the Negro family so ridiculous. How can anyone be responsible without power? Power implies choice. It is not a choice when the options are life or death.

It's against the law of nature to choose death. That's why suicides and soldiers make such interesting subjects. They are going against the laws of nature.

If, however, your father is part of the power group and he does not associate with you then he has chosen not to be your father (and the power group does have this choice). It is then up to you, for your own mental health, to put any ideas of generative father out of your mind and function with your father surrogate. That is, if your Uncle Bill is the one who takes you to the zoo, Uncle Jimmy the one who is there at Christmas and Uncle Steve the one who spends your birthdays with you, then you pull from them the composite father—and though Uncle Albert only loves your mother and doesn't pay much attention to you he should be a part of the composite also. Same with mothers.

If people treat you like a child then you pull together the composite feeling of being mothered. It's illogical to hunger after the love of someone who doesn't love you when there are plenty of people who would love you—if you believe in love—because feeling is a tool that can be used to keep you from having the necessary substance for being a healthy person. As long as we as a people must deal with the no-good-man-loses-a-woman syndrome as an objective reality we will never be able to gather unto ourselves the subjective feelings essential for propelling the actions needed to place the world in its natural order. I have learned these things by living in the world for a quarter-century.

Gus, my father, has always been a fascinating man to me. I haven't always liked him, but then I haven't always liked myself. The two are related. Gus just sort of believes in himself and thinks everything he's done has needed to be done so that he could be the really groovy person he is. My mother usually agrees with him about that. He has functioned as a father, which doesn't mean we always had nifty toys or the latest clothes, but to his mind if he couldn't get it for us we didn't need it anyway. There may be more validity to that than meets the eye. Ultimately my mother took a job which led to many quarrels. They still fuss about it now—only because she wants to quit and he won't let her. Gus, being a great believer in Freud, will probably always have some conflict around him. He'd be lost without it. How can you eliminate conflict without changing the system? Most people want to be comfortable, which is illogical if you're not free. Which is maybe why folks still cut each other up. Conflict is active and must be kept near the surface.

Life/personality must be taken as a total entity. All of your life is all of your life, and no one incident stands alone. Most people evolve. The family and how it's conceptualized have a great effect on anyone. No matter what the feelings, the effect is still there. Like James Baldwin in *Tell Me How Long the Train's Been Gone* still has to negate God and the God influence. God still means something to him. The feeling is still there. Base experiences affect people; before they are born, events happen that shape their lives. My family on my grandmother's side are fighters. My family on my father's side are survivors. I'm a revolutionist. It's only logical. There weren't any times I remember wanting to eat in a restaurant or go to a school that I was blocked from because of color. I don't remember anyone getting lynched. And though I had friends who went to jail during the sit-ins, we were committed to action anyway, so there must have been something deeper. Beliefs generally come through training, and training is based on feeling.

I was trained intellectually and spiritually to respect myself and the people who respected me. I was emotionally trained to love those who love me. If such a thing can be, I was trained to be in power—that is, to learn and act upon necessary emotions which will grant me more control over my life. Sometimes it's a painful thing to make decisions based on our training, but if we are properly trained we do. I consider this a good. My life is not all it will be. There is a real possibility that I can be the first person in my family to be free. That would make me happy. I'm twenty-five years old. A revolutionary poet. I love.

4

A Revolutionary Tale[*]

THE WHOLE DAMN THING is Bertha's fault. Bertha was my roommate and a very Black person, to put it mildly. She's a revolutionary. I don't want to spend needless time discussing Bertha but it's sort of important. Before I met her I was Ayn Rand–Barry Goldwater all the way. Bertha kept asking, how could Black people be conservative? What have they got to conserve? And after a while (realizing that I had absolutely nothing, period) I came around. But not as fast as she was moving. It wasn't enough that I learned to like the regular mass of colored people—as a whole, as it were; she wanted me to like the individual colored people we knew. I resisted like hell but eventually came around. Bertha is the sort of person you eventually come around. ˙

Now, just be patient; you want to know why I'm late, don't you? So I got an Afro and began the conference beat and did all those Black things that we were supposed to do. I even gave up white

* Reprinted from *Negro Digest*, vol. XVII, no. 8, June, 1968, pp. 70–83.

men for the Movement . . . and that was no easy sacrifice. Not that they were that good—nobody comes down with a sister like a brother—but they were a major source of support for me. I agreed that they shouldn't be allowed to support the Movement, but I believe in having income passed around, and if anyone has income to spare, whiteys do. So I cut myself off from a very important love of mine—money—and that presented a problem. No, I'm not going round Robinhood's barn; this is a part of it.

So when my income was terminated for ideological reasons you'd think Bertha would say something like "I'll take over the rent and your gas bill since you've sacrificed so much for the Movement." You'd really think that, wouldn't you? But no, she asked me about a job. A job, for Christ's sake! I didn't even know anybody who worked but her! And here she was talking about a job! I calmly suggested that I would apply for relief. You see, I believe society owes all of its members certain things like food, clothing, shelter and gas, so I was going to apply to society since individual contributions were no longer acceptable. She laughed that cynical laugh of hers and offered to go down with me. "No," says I, "I can do it myself." So I went down at the end of the week.

Now, I'm a firm believer in impressions. I think the first impression people make is very important, and since I would have to consider welfare my job from now on, for Bertha's sake at least, I got dressed up and went down. I'm sure you've applied for relief at least once so you know the procedure. I went to Intake and met an old civil servant, the kind who's been on the job since Hayes set the system up. She asked me so many questions about my personal life I thought she was interviewing me for a possible spot in heaven. Then we got to my family. I told her Mommy was a supervisor in the Welfare Department and Daddy was a social worker. She shook her head and looked disgusted—just plain disgusted with me—huffed up her flat chest and said, "Young lady, you are not eligible for relief!" And stormed away.

I started after her. "What the hell do you mean, 'not eligible'?" I asked. "I'll take somebody's job who really needs it, somebody with skills or the ability to be trained, with a wife and kids, or maybe just an unwed mother will be put out of work! What kind of jive agency are you? You sure don't give a damn about people!" As she turned the corner I had to run to keep up with her. "And who are you to decide what I need? You're nothing but a jive petty bourgeoise bullshit civil servant." Yes, I did. I told her exactly that. I mean, that's what she was. "Going 'round deciding people's needs! You got needs yourself. Who decides how your needs are gonna be filled? You ain't God or Mary or even the Holy Ghost— telling me what I'm eligible for." I was really laying her out. The nerve! I'd come all the way down there and didn't have on Levis or my miniskirt but looked *nice*! I mean really *clean*, and she says I'm not eligible. Really did piss me off.

At the end of the corridor she was hurrying along I saw this figure. It looked small and pitiful. It was Mommy. I guess someone had recognized me and called her to come down. I went over to put my arms around her. "Don't cry, Mommy. It'll be all right." But she just cried and cried and kept saying, "Oh, Kim, why can't you be like other daughters?" I got so involved with soothing her that the servant got away. "Mom," I said as I walked her to her office, "there's going to be a Black Revolution all over the world and we must prepare for it. We've got to determine our own standards of eligibility. That's all." She quit crying a little and just looked at me pitifully. Then she put her arms around me and said, "Oh, Kim, I love you. But why can't you just get married and divorced and have babies and things like other daughters? Why do you have to disgrace us like this? I didn't mind when you got kicked out of school for drinking and I even got used to all those men I didn't like. And remember the time you made the front page for doing that go-go dance at the Democratic Convention? I've been a Democrat all my life! You know that. But I was proud that in the middle of Johnson's speech you jumped on the table, shoes and all, to dance your protest to the war in Vietnam. But this is my job! Your father and I have worked very hard to give you everything we could."

"Mom," I cut her off, "I'm not against your job." I tried to explain it wasn't personal even when I'd had to throw that rock through her window that time. "We didn't firebomb, did we? 'No,' I told the group, 'don't firebomb the Welfare Department.' And when we had to turn the director's car over, you noticed that he didn't get hurt? I told the group, 'Be sure not to hurt the director.' That's what I told them. But Mom, I'm broke now. All my savings are gone and if I don't get on relief I'll have to take a job. Oh, Mommy, what will I do if I take a job? Locked up in a building with all those strangers for eight hours every day. And people saying, 'Good morning, Kim. How's it going?' or 'Hey, Kim, what you doing after work?' I mean, getting familiar with me and I don't even know them! How could I stand that?"

Then, for the first time in the twenty-three years I'd known her, she looked me dead in the eye—I mean exactly straight—and said, "You'll either have to work or go to grad school." It floored me. I mean, she's never made a decision like that all the time I've known her.

"Mom," I said, "you don't mean it. You've been talking to Bertha. You're angry with me for what I told that civil servant. I'll apologize. I'll make it up somehow. I swear! I'll get my hair done!"

But she would not budge. "Kim, it's school or a job."

"Mom, 'member when I went back and graduated from college? Magna cum laude and all. 'Member how proud you and Daddy were that I had the guts to go back after all they did to me in college? 'Member what you said? 'Member how you said I had done *all* you wanted me to do? 'Member how you kept saying you wouldn't ask me for anything else? 'Member, Mom? Mommy? 'Member?"

She still wouldn't budge. I tell you it's something when your own mother turns against you. She knew I was working for the Revolution. "What would happen to the Revolution if I quit to take a job?

What would my people do?" I asked her. And she looked at me and said, rather coldly if I recall, "Your people need you to lead the way. Not just toward irresponsible acts but toward a true Revolution."

"There's nothing irresponsible about chaos and anarchy. We must brush our teeth before eating a meal."

"Kim, I've read everything you have written. I've heard all your speeches on tape. And what are you talking about now? Program. I've read Frantz Fanon and Stokely Carmichael. I especially enjoyed *Burn the Honky* by H. Rap Brown—he's got an amazing sense of humor. I've read Killens and Jones and Neal and McKissick. I've read most of the books on those lists you gave us. Haven't I always tried to understand and sympathize with you? When I was going to get Mother a cookbook, did I buy the *Larousse Gastronomique*? No! I bought the *Ebony Cookbook*, even though Mother has forgotten more than Freda DeKnight could ever have known. When your father and I went to the social work convention in Detroit last year, did we stay with the other delegates at the Hilton? No! We stayed at the Rio Grande. I've done all I could for the Revolution and I'll probably do more. But I'm not going to allow this behavior. You will get a job or you will go to school."

"Aw, Mommy," I protested, "you just don't understand. . . ."

"Kim, that's all there is to it. I'll give you a surprise when you tell me something definite."

I was crushed. Absolutely crushed. My own mother turned against me. I must have looked terribly hurt because she kissed me again and said, "Oh, Kim. It's best—really it is. If I can read your people and try to understand your way, you can try mine."

I called my father. I asked him to take me to lunch. I think he knew. He didn't know when I called him but by the time we met for lunch—he knew. Of course, being a social worker and relating to people and all for a living, he didn't just burst in and say, "I agree with your mother." No. He sat down and ordered me a drink. He doesn't drink anymore since he and his liver made an intellectual decision that Negroes shouldn't get high. This is his sacrifice for the Movement. He'd quit five years earlier when he was in the hospital; he considered it a religious conversion thing. His own special sacrifice to Jesus. We used to ask about it but he always just said Jesus had spoken to him through his liver. And nothing would shake him. He quit church after a couple of months but he continued to tithe every month faithfully and never drank again. His tennis game improved and he got to be a good swimmer again. He took up golf and, to tell the truth, had gotten so damn clean-cut American that Mommy began sneaking gin into his eggs every morning just to keep him from becoming a real bastard. He doesn't know that, however. So we sat down and I had a drink and we ordered lunch.

"What's on your mind, chicken?" (He always calls me some sort of animal or inanimate object. I'm not sure what his message is.)

I didn't want to throw it on him right away. "DaddyMommy-saysI'vegottogotoschoolortakeajobandIdon'tthinkthat'sfair," I said.

"Uhmm. Would you say that again in English . . . I mean American?"

"Mommy says I have to go to school or get a job."

"Good, lambie pie. Which one is it?"

"Daddy, you don't understand. I don't think it's fair."

"Of course not, sugar lump. She shouldn't have said it like that. You just get yourself a nice job. You don't even have to consider school. I'll call up Harry White and see what he can do for you. Or you can get one on your own. . . . You just let me know what you would like."

"Oh, Daddy," I said, "you're on her side and she's been talking to Bertha and nobody even understands me."

"I try to understand you, angel cake. I've read almost all those books on your lists and everything you've written and I've heard all your speeches. I think you're doing fine work but you must set an example, too. You just show your people that new systems can be created. If you want to destroy something, you must first learn how it works and what need it's filling. After the—how do you say —Black Flame encases the world, you'll want your people to work for the Black Nation. How can you encourage that if you have no idea what you're asking of them? That's one thing I noticed about everyone from Nkrumah to Ben Bella to Brown. They don't really know what they're asking everyday people to do. Not that they don't work—and hard—but do they punch a time clock? Do they have a thirty-minute lunch break? Do they dig ditches? Work in a mine? Not that they have to do every one of those; but have they labored? It's important that they do. And all the reading and writing in the world doesn't give a true understanding of time clocks. Maybe they'll do away with time clocks but they must first understand what purpose they serve before they do."

"Oh, Daddy, not that many Black folks ever punch a clock!"

"I'm not talking about a clock and you know it. I'm talking about going to work on time, eating lunch on time, getting off on time, going home on time. All those meetings, conferences and rallies—even if they are on time—are scheduled to your and their convenience, not the people's. Get up at six-thirty or seven, go downtown, eat lunch with a couple of thousand people, relate to your supervisor, relate to your clients, relate to the people in your office or sewer, get off at four-thirty or five, rush home, read your paper while your wife cooks dinner, talk to your children, listen to their troubles, put them to bed; talk to your wife, listen to her troubles, take her to bed; and in your spare time watch TV, say hello to your neighbor, run to the store, go to a rally, try to read a book. Try that and you might understand why the Revolution, as you call it, moves so slowly."

"Oh, Daddy, I didn't want a lecture. I just wanted you to be on my side."

"Is that my name now? Ohdaddy? I am on your side, brown sugar. That's why I'm telling you this. Get yourself a job, then do all the things you're doing. You may readjust your methods."

"I won't change! I won't let the bourgeois system get me!"

"I didn't say your *thinking*, Kim. I didn't say you would readjust your thinking. I said you may change your *methods*."

Lunch was ruined for me. I went home to type a résumé and that wasn't easy. It had been that kind of day.

I have this really neato pink IBM—it was a gift, though when I got it it was a down payment. It's always worked right: I've never had a bit of trouble with it. Once a year I call the people and they clean and service it—that's it. It's a dream. But that day, of all days, it just wouldn't work right. The *s* was skipping and the *a* was hitting twice, plus the magic margin wouldn't click in, and it was just a fucky day. I quit and stretched out on the floor. I fell sort of half-asleep. I couldn't decide between school and an agency job and it must have been on my mind because I had a really terrible dream. There was a university chasing me down the street. I turned the corner to get away from it and ran right into the mouth of an agency. It gobbled me up but it couldn't digest me. When it tried to swallow me I put up such a fight that it belched me back into life. As I hit the street there was the university again, waiting for me like a big dyke with a greasy smile on her lips who has run her prey into a corner. I woke up screaming. Both of them would destroy me! And furthermore, what did I need with a master's degree?

As I brooded on my future the image of educational institutions kept coming back. Going to school is like throwing a rabbit into a brier patch. There would be scores of students I could convert. And because of "academic freedom" the school would have to accept and support me or at least leave me alone unless I flunked out, drank a lot or smoked in public. And if I applied for a job in social work both Mommy and Daddy would be pleased because I'd get a degree and agency training and an inadequate paycheck to boot. So I sat down at my pink IBM to type a letter for an application blank. Surprisingly enough the typewriter was fixed. I mailed it immediately and sat back while others stronger and wiser than I determined my fate.

Geez, you've got a one-track mind! I'm trying to get around to explaining about the delay. I was, you know, accepted in school. I thought everyone would be happy and leave me alone. That was February and I had nine months of Freedom before enrollment day. And I fully intended to use them. I got my acceptance letter on a Tuesday. That was so upsetting that all I could do for a long time was just gnash and growl. It didn't bother Bertha a bit. She just started running around the house singing, "Kim's going to school. . . ." You know, like she was happy. My mood wasn't too positive so I told her, dead calmly, that if she didn't get the hell out of my half of the apartment I'd kill her. She laughed one of those grand ha-ha-ha-type things, then spread her arms and pir- ouetted out the door.

It was hard to take. After these years of freedom of choice and movement I was going back to school. I just cried and cried. Then I thought: what the hell! Hadn't I survived the time we were play- ing "The Prince of Wales"? Hadn't I survived the Wisconsin Sleeper? Hadn't I been to Harlem? Hadn't I refused to lay a white boy when we were in Mississippi on the big march? Why wouldn't I survive now? I was really talking it up to myself. Much worse things had happened to me and here I was acting like a crybaby. Why wouldn't I survive, I asked myself bravely, boldly—perhaps brazenly! Why would I not survive? BECAUSE! Came the answer and I cried and cried.

I've got to tell you this. No, don't be that way—listen. If ever something happens to you that makes you really unhappy and you've just got to cry about it, don't cry in the same spot. Move around. That's what I learned. After I cried and cried, there was this shiny puddle around my feet and there were these blood-red eyes looking up at me. I learned then, never cry in one spot. But I was cool with it. I never really got emotionally involved in it. I cleaned up the mess, took a shower, got dressed to a T, then went out walking the streets.

I stopped by a bar I know and had a drink. One of my brothers, soul brothers, bought me a drink and we started discussing what would have to come down. He and I got into a real deep thing and we talked until the bar closed. He kept wanting to kill Toms and I still think that's not who we have to kill. Toms, I told him, only have power if we let them have power. I mean, if a Tom says get off the streets and you get off the streets, then that's your fault, not his. If on the other hand a Tom tells you to get off the streets and you don't—well, then the power structure has no use for him. Plus if you can encourage him in a physical way to come on over to your side, you've made a friend. I mean, you can beat a brother or boycott him or something besides killing him to get him to either help you or get out of the way. There are too few brothers on this shore already for them to be killing each other off. We need to get rid of whitey. I mean, if we can't kill a whitey, how can we ever justify killing a brother? That's a hell of a copout to me. Talking about killing brothers—and sisters too—and not being able to kill a whitey. We can only justify offing a brother if we have already offed twenty whiteys—that's the ratio, I told him, for offing a brother. So we went to his place to talk further.

The next morning all my problems were solved, I thought. I had figured it all out. Now, this much I knew about social work school— they will put up with anything at all except heterosexual relations. I mean, anything at all. And the school where I was accepted was founded by two ladies who had adopted children. I just knew if I wrote them and explained that I had not only been screwing but had enjoyed it—well, I thought, they'd write a nice letter explaining the mistake in accepting me and that would be the end of that. So I jumped up and dashed home to compose a letter. Then I thought, that won't get to them soon enough—I'd better send a wire. So I did.

PLEASE BE ADVISED STOP I HAVE SCREWED STOP IT WAS GOOD
STOP SO THERE EXCLAMATION POINT YOURS IN FREEDOM

KIM

I thought they would really be sick of me the minute they received that. I got a long, involved letter explaining how proud they
were that I was open to new things and that they were very
pleased at my level of honesty. I tell you I was p. oed. That's the
only way to describe it. And what the hell did she mean, "new
things"? I'd been screwing since I was twelve—ten if you want to
count the times before it was serious. And he wasn't new anyway.
I was truly indignant, but Bertha discouraged me from expressing
my feelings to the school by just demoralizing my whole intellectual thing.

Well, yes, it was a calculated intellectual involvement. You see,
I never act on my unbridled emotions. Emotions are to be controlled by the intellect. Even when I act in what could be considered an emotional manner, I have thought it out before and have
decided this will be the way I act. So to have my whole intellectual
bag blown sky high right before my eyes—well, that was frightening. I started to give Bertha a quick punch in the gut but my whole
action-reaction syndrome began to reek of emotion so I just cooled
it a bit and dropped a half-teaspoon of Drano in her coffee later
during the day.

Strange about that. I was only playing a little joke and there
was plenty of milk on hand, you see, to help offset the effects. So
Bertha drank her coffee and went to the john and never once
indicated that anything was wrong. Later, when I asked, she did
say it had been awfully runny, but that was all. I'm a failure, I told
myself—a failure. Oh, goody! I'm a failure. I don't have to deal
with it anymore. I dashed another telegram off to the director of
placement:

PLEASE BE ADVISED STOP HAVE PUT DRANO IN ROOMMATES
COFFEE STOP SHE LIVES STOP I AM A FAILURE STOP YOU MUST
REJECT ME STOP

Those ridiculous people up there just considered it a bid for attention. I got a nice, long letter explaining how they realized I hadn't received an answer to my application yet and they were sorry but they had a lot of work and sometimes even the best of us get tied up, etc. Plus, if you can dig it, they thought I had ingenious ways of letting them know my needs. I mean, really! Ingenious! Goddammit, I was a failure. If I didn't find a quick way out of this, why I'd end up in an institution, a part of an agency, being decent, responsible—all those ugly, sick things that I hated. I'd really have to think of a scheme.

It was way in the middle of April before it even dawned on me. I mean, it was so simple; I was overlooking the obvious. What is the one thing we know for damned sure about white people? I mean, you know, besides the fact that they hate Negroes, children and sex. . . . What is the one thing we know absolutely and positively about any honkie anywhere in the world? That he worships money. He's got such a case about money he's transferred it to anything green. That's why you see those goddamn "KEEP OFF THE GRASS" signs. Not that he cares about grass, but it's green. What's the quickest way to turn a honkie off? Ask him for money. He's as nice as he can be as long as he thinks he'll get your money—but the minute you ask him for some, well, that's like asking a hippie for his pot or a Negro for his knife. I mean, they get *hostile*. You don't believe it? Go into any bank and deposit five bucks. Then go back in a week and withdraw it. When you go to deposit it they're all smiles. A V.P. will come out and shake your hand. The teller smiles and welcomes you to the family. And that's only five bucks I'm talking about. When you go to withdraw it, the first thing the teller will say is, "You realize this will close your account." Just like you didn't know that if you deposit five bucks and you withdraw five bucks you are closing your account. And you just smile at him and say, "Yea, groovy." He'll frown and say, "This will cost you one dollar." And you say, "Cool. Gimme my four bucks." Then he says, "This will take a minute." That's when you look at him very menacingly and say, "I should surely hope the hell not." Then he'll slam your money down and scream, "NEXT," or he'll slap the "NEXT WINDOW PLEASE" sign up and turn his back on you. And this is a Black teller I'm talking about.

So, knowing this, I wrote the director of placement and told her I had no money and needed a stipend and a tuition grant. I just knew, whatever my charm or what not, they weren't going to pay me to go to their school. I mean, as tight as they are, they are not about to give me any money. I was as happy as a ten-year-old turkey the day before Thanksgiving. I knew I now had them by the ass—I was just naturally too tough to handle. I walked a little taller, breathed a little deeper, felt a little prouder. I was so happy that I went back to my Revolution work. Not that I hadn't been working for the Revolution all along, but I had really been hung up on this thing about a job.

We set up a Black Arts Festival and I was working my you-know-what off. You may have heard about me being on the radio telling all the honkies not to come. I'm sure you heard about Lonnie going into the honkie neighborhood with his sign saying, "YOU'RE NOT READY." It was great advertising for us and we were all really sorry about that kid. However, though the papers played it down after the first day it is not true that Lonnie tore his leg from the joint—he only fractured it. And contrary to first reports the kid will walk again. I personally tell all the brother Black Belts I know that they shouldn't provoke white kids, then beat on them. But, well, you're not always able to control folks, even if they do take a lot of your advice. But that was the only incident that could be, in some quarters, considered unfortunate. It was a groovy set. The blue beasts foamed at the mouth but it was our day! I say again, it was revolutionary! Slavetown, U.S.A., was back in the Movement 'cause the Kim was back into her thing.

I really forgot all that crap about school and jobs and do. I just put it out of my mind. Our underground press, yes, it does have something to do with why I'm late. You see, we were putting out a magazine called *Love Black*. It was a group thing, you know, but it really belonged to all the people. We had learned the secret of why the folks don't read. C'mon, see do you know. You jive, they can *too* read. But nobody ever writes for them or writes anything they can relate to. So, having figured that out through the very difficult process of stopping every brother we could on the corner one day and asking him what he would enjoy reading, we went about getting *Love Black* out. See, most folks don't read, honkies especially, but people too. You think they really read *Good Housekeeping* or *Time?* They look at the pictures and will scan an article they can see the end of. Most people like to read what they can see the end of. So we started a Black mag on 8½- by 11-inch paper, with articles that took up a page or less. Also, it didn't run more than twenty pages all toto. Therefore, a brother could read the whole damned mag and really do two things: learn something positive about himself, and complete something he started.

Now, don't start breaking into my explanation. It may well have been propaganda but all pieces of paper with writing are propaganda, and if I have to deal in mind control it's much better to be Blackwashed. I mean, the honkie press just naturally screws with any Black man's mind because it doesn't recognize that there is a Black mind. It does what it can to a Black mind—it whitewashes it, it flushes it out of his head. That's what it does. But we were giving the people something and we were getting a lot. One issue we were late and all kinds of soul stepped up and told me if I didn't get my thing together and get the mag out, well, they would look upon that with disfavor. And they also sent articles in. Like we'd get slightly used toilet tissue with an article on it, or brown paper bags with short sayings, or just a note to say the writer dug us. Some of it looked like our ancestral writing and we really had to work at deciphering it, but when you saw how the man changed after he had "published," well, it would really hit you. You see, the brother will read if he's writing it or if he knows people who are, and *Love Black* was strictly ours. It wasn't the prettiest thing in the world and sometimes it wasn't too clear. I've always maintained that if the Revolution fails it'll be because we know nothing about machinery. But it was ours. It talked about Slavetown and what the brother thought and felt, and the brother was digging it. You got to understand the whole concept of writing.

On the East Coast everything is dishonest. They do a lot of things but mostly it's 3,000 percent bullshit. The people are so used to talking Black, buying Black and thinking Black they don't get shook anymore. Every hustler (why is it a Black capitalist is called a hustler?) and every panhandler is Black, so Black doesn't mean anything. It's taken for granted. And one Black thing is like another. They've been saturated with a program that has never come off. Between Garvey and Malcolm, Harlem should be owned lock, stock and barrel by us—but we are still trying to get rat control and jobs, and paying rent to honkies.

In the DuPont plantation state they even passed a law that said if building codes aren't lived up to you can deposit your money in one of the company banks and leave it there till the cat comes around. Ain't that the jivest crap you ever heard of? I mean, paternalism with a capital WHITE. No, wait a minute. If you live in a house or apartment and something is wrong with it, and you are living there every day the good Lord makes you Black, well, you should fix that place up and what's left over from rent should go in your pocket. So the old witch from the Welfare Department comes down and tries to explain that she'll have to hold your check if you don't pay your rent to the rightful owner. And that's when you come out of your thing so righteously and whip it on her so beautifully. You just light up a joint and calmly explain that "Honkies have made women, bombs and Kellogg's corn flakes, but they have never made a piece of land. The land is one bitch that is everybody's woman and I, being a man and all, have got a right to a piece of her."

You see, the honkies' whole sex thing is tied up to land. No lie. Land is their love. All land, except Germany, is female. The motherland, her, she—all land is woman. And they do anything to prove that they are worthy to be land's man. Only land doesn't give a crap about white people. See, land has this memory thing. Land remembers God stepped out in space and looked around and said, "I'LL MAKE ME A MAN." God reached down into land, a woman, and formed this thing—you know, a man. Now, land has always been Black. And you know God well enough to know that he goes first class. So God got the best land he could find, which had to be the Blackest land he could find. You just don't know about any white land. Snow, maybe, some white sand, maybe; but you just don't know about any white land. And land is hip to that. Land is very put out that we are making her prostitute herself for the beast. You didn't hear about any land being raped until the beast came along.

We live in harmony with land because we are part of land and we are out of land. The honkie came from sand and snow. Now, what are they? They're nothing. They have a place on earth but they're nothing. Snow freezes land and sand dries her up; both destroy land and land wants to live and re-create. You run it on down to where you are going to free land so that she can go about woman's work of taking care of her children—the Black people of the earth. Now, she'll send the law out but that doesn't mean anything either. The law only means something if you think it does. So she'll send out the law to make you pay and you smile sincerely and promise to get it in next week. After you're alone with your piece of land you remove very carefully anything that cannot be replaced, like pictures of your first lay, your joints, etc., and you throw kerosene on everything else. You see, it's yours, and if you can't enjoy it in freedom and peace, then land wants you to destroy it.

You can't destroy land because she'll always be there, but you can destroy the rapist's claim. The only thing about land that makes the beast think he owns her is the stake he's put up to clinch his claim—a house, a building, a fence—so you destroy that. That's when you burn. You don't burn to get the thief to fix it up; you burn when you've staked your claim and they try to steal it from you. And I really believe that after you've fixed it up and made it yours, you'll kill for it.

That's the thing we've got to understand. The Revolution isn't to show what we're willing to die for; Black people have been willing to die for damned near everything on earth. It's to show what we're willing to kill for. Yes, it is! Do we love life enough to deal righteously with key honkies? We don't have to deal with King and Young and those other three or four if we don't want to. We have got to deal with the folks who sent them up. Which means we have to control ourselves. I have got to control me and you have got to control you. If I see something that needs to be done and you see something else, we don't have to argue about what to do. You do yours and I'll do mine. It's like we're on a road that forks and then comes back together. We just had different priorities, and that don't make one right or wrong—just different. But if I use the fact that you want to do something I don't want to do to keep from doing what I have to do, then I'm not together. I'm bullshitting and I know it.

You and I are never in a conflict situation because we're after the same thing—we're after the same honkie—and however we get him is our business. All that jive about coordination and keeping people in line and élites is crap and doesn't really mean anything. That's no Revolution—that's not anarchy! And anarchy is what we want. This country doesn't even have anything that we can't build again if we need it. Even to try to think of taking over and preserving General Motors—what for? Nobody's trying to make the system Black; we're trying to make a system that's human so that Black folks can live in it. This means we're trying to destroy the existing system. It's not even a question of whether Black folks can run it better than white folks. We don't have to prove to whiteys that we can—and if we took over their system it would be for that reason. We haven't got to prove anything to honkies because they are nobody's authority on anything.

But the whole damn thing I do blame on Bertha, because I was just happy sitting at home twiddling my toes and masturbating every now and then. I didn't even know that I was colored, let alone anything about Blackness. But she kept bringing those beautiful Black people home and they kept talking that talk to me, and as I moved I moved toward Black Power. And I recognized the extent of white power, which is so pervasive that the American solution cannot be Black Power at all, though as a world solution it is a possibility. It must be Revolution—anarchy, total chaos—and this should not be so hard for us since we have worked so diligently in every other cause; we can now work for our own. We have sacrificed our lives and interests for white power; now we can save ourselves through Revolution—our baptism by fire.

But as I worked this out, people kept calling me a hater, and really I'm a lover. No one knows how much I do love all that is lovable. Then Bertha chimed in to ask whether I love Black folks enough to trust them to TCB, and whether I trust black people to do those things necessary by any means necessary, recognizing that the means are in fact the ends. She kept saying that if they and I are one then I should get out of the way and see where they would go without me. And since Revolution ages you so quickly, and having watched the summer, I had to admit that I was old and tired, and I recognized that already we were moving beyond my vision. Maybe I should step aside and regroup.

So I packed and made arrangements to come to school, and everybody cheered and was really pleased with my decision. And I kept telling myself that it would be good and that I was dealing with the best the system had to offer and that, if I couldn't relate meaningfully enough to them to accept them, then I could easily go back to destroying it in a very real manner.

Having made my decision, I decided to walk. I mean, it would have been much too easy to hop a flight or thumb a ride. And though physical punishment of myself didn't span the whole import of my act, it did serve as a human extension of myself to help offset my total feelings of wasting my time. Then or now.

And I had no idea you are so far away from Uncle Tom's Cabin in Slavetown. I thought I could make it in a day or two but it's taking much longer. I'm really sorry about holding you up and all, but it's done now and here I am. See can you handle it.

5

*Don't Have a Baby
till You Read This*

WELL, YOU SEE, I hadn't talked with you, that is, you weren't born and I wasn't expecting you to be. So I decided to spend Labor Day with my parents in Cincinnati. Now, when I told my doctor, because you didn't have a doctor yet, that I was going, he thought that I was going to fly, he told me later, though he couldn't have really thought that because airlines won't let you fly in the last month. But anyway he wasn't thinking and neither to tell the truth was I. So I started out in Auntie Barb's new convertible Volkswagen and we all know how comfortable they are when you plan to drive 800 miles. But that's really not important.

We actually got started about 7:00 A.M. so that we could beat the morning traffic. When we hit the Pennsylvania Turnpike, I thought that was the turning point. We had stopped for lunch before the long stretch into West Virginia when this big black car went zoooooming past us and this thing fell out. I thought, how awful that those white people in the *passing lane* would be throwing out garbage. Then it became obvious that it wasn't and I said,

God, I'm gonna hit that dog that fell out of that car, and just as I was adjusting to that Barb said, "IT'S A CHILD!" and I hit the brakes and luckily so did the truck driver in the middle lane and I hopped out of the car while the truck stopped. And the father ran back saying, "Oh, my God! Oh, my God!" but the mother just sat in the car and didn't even turn around and the other small child, another little girl, just looked back to see and maybe there was a glint in her eye, but it's hard to tell under excited circumstances. And Barb said, "What cha doing getting out of the car? What if that truck hit you?" And I thought it would be a terrible thing for an evil militant like me to be hit on the turnpike because some white people threw their child out the window the way they throw their cats in the lake and I vowed it would never happen to me again. But you were inside and you stirred and I said, "Emma," because I called you Emma, thinking that you were going to be a girl, and I was naming you after your great-grandmother, "I'll never throw you out the car 'cause we don't treat our children that way."

And Barb was so upset by the whole thing that she asked me if I wanted her to drive. Barb was always that way. She figures if she's upset then everybody is more upset than she is because she thinks she's so cool and all. But knowing that about her I drove until we hit Athens, Ohio, and she brought us in into Cincy.

When we walked into the house my mother—since you weren't born she was still just my mother—said, "When you gonna have that thing? You look like you're gonna have it any minute!" And being modern and efficient and knowing she doesn't know anything about having children, I said, "Oh, Mother, the baby isn't due until the middle of September. And I don't look like that." She was walking around the house all bent over backwards with her flat tummy poking out and laughing at me. Your Aunt Gary laughed at me also but I reminded her she hadn't had a baby in ten years and things had changed since then. Plus I was tired so I said I was going to bed and Gary said, "Why not spend the night with us since we'll have to go to the store tomorrow for the weekend?" And I said the way Mommy was treating me I should go somewhere because it was obvious she wasn't going to let up, so I said, "Emma and I will spend the night with Gary."

At which Gary said, "You're having a boy and we ought to decide on a name for him." You know how group-oriented Gary is. So she called everyone and said, "*We* have to name Nikki's baby." I said, "Her name is Emma. But I don't have a middle name for her." And we kicked that around. Then Gus came upstairs—he always goes downstairs when all his women come home for some reason—and said, "You know, my father's name was Thomas." And I said, "Well, if it's a boy we'll name him Thomas." And the reason I could be so easy about saying I'd name a Black child in 1969 Thomas was that I knew you'd be a girl. So we settled the name thing and I went and had an extended B.M., and I thought that junk on the turnpike really shaped my constipation up. And really, which you may remember, I thought you were constipation all through the first four months, so it wasn't unusual that I still thought that. Your very first foods were milk of magnesia and Epsom salts because I kept thinking I was a little stopped up. And when I didn't get regular I started the sitting-up exercises because I thought I was in bad shape and getting too fat for the laxatives to work. And to tell the truth I didn't think of being pregnant until we were in Barbados and the bikini suit stretched under my tummy and I told Barb, "I think I'm going to have a baby, Barb." And she said she had suspected as much.

So we went out to Gary's to spend the night and Barb went to Grandma Kate's and Mommy and Gus had to stay all by themselves. And the next morning I was tired but I had been tired so long I hopped out of bed with Chris, who offered to fix me one of those good cheese, dried ham and turkey sandwiches that he fixes for breakfast, and I had to turn the little guy down and settle for tea. Chris asked, "Are you really gonna have a baby?" and I said, "It looks like that." And he said, "Is it hard?" And I said, "I don't know much about it but Emma probably knows what to do." And he said, "Well, I'm glad to have my own first cousin 'cause every-body else has first cousins. But I wish you'd have a boy." And I said, "It's really out of my hands, Chris." And he smiled that Chris smile that says you-really-could-do-it-if-you-wanted-to-but-you-don't and said, "If you have a boy I can give him all my old clothes and teach him how to swim and give him my football helmet." And I said, "I think it's going to be a girl. But we don't have to worry about that now." So he went to wake his mother up so we could go to the grocery store. Gary came to breakfast saying, "Chris really wants you to have a boy 'cause most of his friends have brothers and since he doesn't he's got nobody to fight with him." And I said, "Gary, why don't you have a baby or talk to Barb or Mommy? Because I'm going to have a girl." And she gave me that Gary smile that says you-really-could-do-it-if-you-wanted-to-but-you-don't and said, "Well, I don't see why Chris never gets any-thing he wants from this family. He's part of it like anyone else." And we went to the store.

You know Gary's sense of organization, so all her friends and Mommy and Gus came over that night to fix the food for Labor Day. And we were up late playing bid whist because I love bid whist and since most of my friends are ideologists we rarely have time for fun. But I was winning when I told A.J., my brother-in-law, "I think I'll call it a day." And I went to lie down. Gary came back and said, "Are you in labor?" And I said, "Of course not. The baby isn't coming until the middle of September." And I stretched out. Then Barb came back and said, "Are you having pains?" And I said, "No, I'm not, 'cause the baby isn't coming until the middle of September and that's two weeks away and I'm just tired and a little constipated. Maybe I should take a laxative." And she said, "Just stretch out." Then I heard Gus tell Mommy, "You better go see about Nikki. Those children don't know anything about babies." And Mommy, who usually prefers not to be involved, said, "They know what they're doing." But he prodded her with "*What kind of mother are you?* The baby's back there in pain and all *you* care about is your bid!" So she came back and tenderly said, "Your father thinks you're going to have the baby. Are you all right?" And I said, "Of course. I'm just a little constipated." And she asked if I wanted a beer. "When I was pregnant with Gary I drank beer a lot and it helped." So I said yes to pacify her and I heard Gus say, "You're giving the baby a *BEER?* Lord, Yolande! You're gonna *kill* the child!" And she said something real soft and everybody laughed and Mommy didn't come back.

Then the house was quiet and I still didn't feel well and I kept thinking if I could just use the bathroom it would all be OK, but I couldn't use the bathroom. So I was pacing back and forth and Chris came out and said, "Are you having the baby?" and I said no. And Gary came out and said, "It may have been ten years but I think you're having the baby." And I said, "Don't be ridiculous. I paid my hospital bill in New York and I'm not having the baby here." And she said, "OK, but I'm going to call Barb 'cause you've been up all night." And I said, "It's only 3:00 A.M. and don't wake anybody up. I'm not having the baby. It's the junk I ate on the turnpike." But she called Barb, who said, "Maybe we better call Dr. Burch in New York because he would know." And I said, "Don't call him and wake him up. I'm not having any baby." But she did. Dr. Burch said I wasn't having the baby until the first of October according to his calculations but to take me to the hospital anyway to be sure and to let him know no matter what time. And that was when I first realized that he really cared and he said to tell me not to worry because it's a simple thing and I thought, uh-huh. And poor A.J. was awakened to take me. They said I wouldn't be in labor until the water broke but to keep an eye on it. So everybody went back home to bed and Barb slept on the couch.

Around six I noticed I was still up and I was really tired and I started crying and saying, "If I just understood what's wrong I would feel better!" And Barb said, "You're probably going to have the baby." And I said, "No, Barb. You know I'm not until the middle of September." And she said, "Burch says the first of October so you both may be off." "Emma," I said, "you wouldn't do this to me." But you didn't move. I had started to the toilet for the umpteenth time when I wet on myself and I was so embarrassed that I felt like a fudgecicle on a hot day or a leaf in autumn. I just wanted to get it over with. So Barb whispered something to Gary who told A.J. and the next thing I knew I was on my way to the hospital again. This time they said, "Take her right on in." And the doctor came to check me and said, "Take her right on upstairs." Then he smiled at me: "You're going to have a baby."

"A BABY? BUT I DON'T KNOW ANYTHING ABOUT HAVING A BABY! I'VE NEVER HAD A BABY BEFORE." And I started crying and crying and crying. What if I messed up? You were probably counting on me to do the right thing and what did I know? I was an intellectual. I thought things through. I didn't know shit about action. I mean, I could follow through in group activities, I could maybe even motivate people, but this was something I had to do all by myself and you were counting on me to do it right. Damn, damn, damn. Why me?

When in doubt, I've always told myself, be cool and positive. Like when they said God was dead and Forman asked for his money back, I said, "God was a good fellow when he was around." You know what I mean—the moderate statement. When L.B.J. decided not to run for president again I said, "That's good." You know? There's something positive in everything. We've got to keep things balanced. So when they wheeled us upstairs and I immediately understood it was you and me and I wasn't going to be much good crying, I stopped and went to sleep.

"SHE WENT TO SLEEP? IN THE MIDDLE OF LABOR?" my mother said. And she came right out to the hospital. But there wasn't anything she could do so she just sat down and had a beer with one of the ambulatory patients. The nurse woke me up and asked how I felt and I said fine because I didn't want to upset her with my troubles. And I tried to go to sleep again. I had been up all night and was quite tired. Then the doctor came and said, "Bear down when you have pain." So I grunted. And he said, "Are you in pain now?" And I said I didn't want him to think I was being negative but I wasn't in pain until he stuck his hand up there. And he told the nurse, "Maybe we better take the baby. Get her doctor on the phone." So they called Burch and he said, "You better take the baby if she's sleeping because that is a bad sign." And they told me what he'd said. Then this cherubic woman came in and said, "I'm your anaesthesiologist and I'm going to give you a spinal." Then she began explaining all the various things about it and I said, "Under more normal circumstances I'm sure this would be very interesting. But right now if you'd just like to go ahead and do it it would be fine with me. I mean, I really trust the hospital a lot right now and I'm sure you're more than qualified." She looked at me rather perplexedly and I was going to suggest we meet in the cafeteria the next day when I don't remember anything more. Then there was this blinding light and the doctor said, "We'll have to give you a Caesarean," and I said I knew that when I realized I was pregnant or at least I wanted to. And he said, "We'll give you a bikini cut," and I tried to explain that I didn't GIVE A DAMN what they gave me, just get the baby. And the bikini cut didn't work because then I heard, "Nurse, he won't come out this way. We'll have to give her. . . ." I decided: when in doubt. . . . Then he said, "I think we've got him," and I opened my eyes because I wanted to know what you looked like in case they misplaced you or something and there you were, butt naked and really quite messy, and they said, "Mother"—why do they call people that?—"you've got a boy." And I thought, but I was having a girl. Then I went to sleep for a good rest.

When I woke up I thought it was the next day, only it was the day after that. And people kept coming around saying, "She looks much better." I thought, God, I must be really fine, so I asked the floor nurse for a mirror and she said, "Be right back," but she wasn't. Then I noticed a line running into my arm and one out of my leg and it dawned on me I must look like hell on a stick. And I thought it behooved me to ask about my condition. The nurses all said, "You're fine now, Mother," and I said, "My name is Nikki," and they said, "Yes, Mother." So when Gary came I was interested in how I had done. And she, typical of hospital personnel, said, "You're much better now." So I said, "How was I then?" "A good patient." And I said, "Gary, when I get up I'm gonna kill you if you don't tell me." "Well, you would have come through with flying colors if your heart hadn't stopped. That gave the doctors some concern for a while. Then the baby—he's cute; did you know he was sucking his thumb in the incubator? The smartest little guy back there. Well, he was lying on your bladder and a piece of it came out. But other than that you're fine. Mommy and Gus and Barb and I were with you all the time." And I thought, uh-huh. "And Chris is really glad you had a boy. He said he knew you could do it if you wanted." And I thought, uh-huh.

Then she had to leave the floor because the babies were coming. I pulled my gown straight and worked my way into a sitting position and smiled warmly like mothers are supposed to do. And the girl next to me got her baby. Then all the people on my side. Then all the people on the other side. And I started to cry. The floor nurse said, "What's the matter, Mother?" and I cried, "Something has happened to my baby and nobody will tell me about it." And she said, "No. Nursery didn't know you were well. I'll go get it for you." And I said, "Him. It's a boy." So she brought you to me and Gary was right. Undoubtedly the most beautiful, intelligent, everything baby in the world. You had just finished eating so we sat, you in your bassinet and me in my bed, side by side. Then the nurse said, "Don't you want to hold him?" And I started to say, bitch, holding is to mothers what sucking is to babies what corners are to prostitutes what evasion is to politicians. But I just looked at her and she looked at the lines into and out of me so she put you in the bed, and you were very quiet because you knew I didn't feel too swell and if you did anything I wouldn't be able to help you.

The next morning my doctor came by and said his usual and I said, "I guess so I'm alive," and he said, "If you'll eat I'll take the tube out of your arm." Remembering what hospital food had been like when I'd had my hemorrhoidectomy a couple of years back, I hesitated, but he reminded me that I could feed you so I was suckered. And I was glad because I met the dietician, who was really a wonderful woman. But I made the mistake of saying I liked oatmeal and she made the mistake of giving me a lot and I didn't eat it, and they said, "Mother, if you don't eat we'll have to put the tube back in." So I had to tell her to keep my diet thing together. Institutions make it hard for you to make friends. Then someone asked if I wanted you circumcised and I said yes and they brought you back and you were maaaad. And I loved it because you showed a lot of spirit. And I snuck you under the covers and we went to sleep because we'd both had a long, hard day. They said you wouldn't let the nurse in white touch you for a good long time after that, which is what I dig about you—you carry grudges. And that was a turning point. I decided to get you out of there before they got your heart.

It's a funny thing about hospitals. The first day I was really up and around they were having demonstrations on how to avoid unwanted pregnancies, and I really was quite interested but since I was from New York and in their opinion didn't belong on the ward they called everyone who was ambulatory together and left me in the bed. Then they privately visited the catheterized patients, of whom I was still one, and they passed me by with one of those smiles nurses give you. And the aides came over and one said, "I understand you teach school. What are you doing on the ward?" And I said, "I teach school and I'm here to have the baby." "But you're from New York." And failing to see the connection I said, "I'm Gary's little sister," and they said, "Oh." But since they never thought of me as being a poor Black unwed mother I didn't get any birth control lessons. Hospitals carry the same inclinations as the other institutions.

That Wednesday they brought you to me for the morning feeding and you, being impatient and hungry, were crying all the way. When I heard the wail, I knew it was you and it was. You cried and cried and I was struggling to get you up in the bed and you didn't care anything at all about the problems Mommy was having. Finally I got you in and fed you and you smiled. I swear you did, just before I put the bottle in. Well, I had pulled the curtain so we could be alone and I guess they forgot about us because when they came to get the babies they left you. And I sat and watched you sleeping. Then I started crying and crying and Gary came in and caught me. "What's the matter with you?" she sympathetically asked and I said, "He's so beautiful," and I cried a little longer and she said, "You sure are silly," looked at you and then said, "He really is beautiful, almost as pretty as Chris," and I thought, uh-huh.

She left to get me some cigarettes and I decided to sit all the way up so I could cuddle you, and for some reason I started feeling real full but I knew I didn't have to use the bathroom because I was catheterized, so I paid it no mind. Gary brought the cigs back and I lit up my first cigarette since coming to the hospital. Then it happened. The bed was flooded with urine. And I with great exactitude said, "NURRRSE," and she came running. "What's the matter, Mother? What are you doing with the baby still here?" *"Never mind that! I've wet the bed."* And she laughed and laughed. "You're the only catheterized patient in my knowledge who ever wet the bed." Then she called someone to change it. The aide laughed too and said, "What's the baby doing still in here?" And I made up my mind to ask the doctor as soon as he came.

"What do I have to do to get out of here?" "What's the rush? You can take your time." "I wanna go home." "To New York? That'll be a long time." "To my mother's." "Well, if you can walk and use the bathroom, we'll let you out Sunday. But I don't think you should worry about that." "I'll be ready."

So the first thing I had to do was get out of bed. I hadn't been out of bed since I got in because I had peeped a couple of days before that the position I was in was the critical position. The woman on the other side in number 1 had been moved but I had stayed. People had moved into number 2 but I was still in 1. And I guess if they had told me how sick I was when I was that sick, I would have died. So in the interest of not upsetting God I just lay back and did what they told me to. Now I had to get up so I could get you home.

First I got the bag and flung my legs over the side. Then I smoked a cigarette to congratulate myself. Then I stood up. And I must say the world had changed considerably since I had lain. Everything was spinning. But you know me. If there's a challenge, I'll overcome. So I moved on to the chair. I was huffing and puffing like I had just felled a tree or climbed a mountain, and I was scared. What if I fell and they decided to keep me there for another week or so? But I made it into the chair and sat up. My timing was perfect. The nurse who messed with stitches came by and smiled. "Oh, you're sitting up?" And I said sure with a smile, hoping she wouldn't see the sweat I was working up. "Maybe I'd better get back in bed so you can examine me" (rather hopefully put out), and she said it would be better. Well, at least I had done the first thing.

That evening I sat up for a delicious dinner of warm milk (just to room temperature), gray goo and green goo. They smiled and said, "It'll make you strong," and I thought about my mother saying the same thing about Father John's medicine and I thought, uh-huh.

You can tell a lot about a woman from the way she masturbates. Some go at it for a need thing, some because their hand just happened to hit it, some to remember their childhood. Some women turn on their backs, some their stomachs, some their sides. You can peep a whole game from that one set. So in the interest of finding what was left and what wasn't I reached down to this skinned chicken and said to myself, yeah, it's still there but good and tired.

And it wasn't in the mood for any games. I felt the necessity to check since every stranger in the world it seemed had looked up my legs. Institutions still haven't found a way to give service and leave the ego intact. Realizing for one that I hadn't needed to be shaved and for two never having been very hairy, I got nervous and wanted my mother. "Will it grow back?" I asked and she said sure, it always does. But it had taken me a good nineteen years of brushing and combing and high-protein diet to get the little I had and maybe it'd take that long to grow back. "Certainly not. It'll be there before you know it," but I still worried. I wanted to get out of there before they shaved my head and took my kidney.

The next thing, since I had so easily mastered sitting up, was walking down to the nursery and back. I made that my goal since I would have you as a reward at the end and the bed at the return. As I stepped lightly from my bed and grabbed my bag, flung my pink robe in grand style over my shoulders and started from position 1 to the nursery, I heard a collective gasp go up in the ward —"Ooooooo"—and I smiled, waved my hand a little and then proceeded. Visions of the old house flew before my face. We lived now in an all-Black city called Lincoln Heights. It wasn't our first real home but it was our first house. When we'd gotten that house we'd all been very excited because I would have a yard to play kickball in, Gary would have a basement to give parties in, Mommy would have a real living room and Gus would have peace and quiet. It was ideal. And we all could make all the noise we wanted to. I have always thought it's very important for people to have their own piece of land so that they can argue in peace and quiet. Like when we had rented an apartment, we hadn't really been able to have arguments and Mommy and Daddy had had to curse each other out on Saturday afternoons so that the landlady wouldn't complain. But now they could fight all day long and well into the night without disturbing anyone. And Gus could throw things and Mommy could call him a motherfucker without appearing to be crude. People need something all to themselves.

I was halfway down the aisle. I passed the fifteen-year-old who had cried, "Help me," because she hadn't known how to feed her baby. I was quickly approaching the thirty-five-year-old who had had the twelve-pound baby. I was going past the girl who listened to "I Can't Get Next to You" all day long on her godawful radio.

We had lived in the old house until I was seventeen; Mommy and I had decided that she and Gus made enough money to have a new house. "I ain't moving" was Gus's reply to our loving suggestion. "I'm happy where I am. A man gets comfortable in his house and the next thing you know they want him to move." And we began looking for houses in Lincoln Heights because we didn't want to lay too much on him at one time. I mean, my father is an old man and it's been proved that old people die earlier when they are uprooted. Like my grandmother would probably have lived another ten or twenty years, but urban renewal took her home that she had lived in for forty-three years, and she was disjointed and lost her will to live. Like a lot of other old folks. I guess nobody likes to see memories paved over into a parking lot. It just doesn't show respect.

So we found a nice little home on the other side of Lincoln Heights and mentioned to my father how we were closing the deal and would be moving in a month. "Nikki, you and your mother can do what you want. She never did listen to me anyway. But I'm staying here." "But you'll be all alone." "Nope. I'll have my radio and I can listen to the ball games. I don't need any of you." "But we need you, Gus. What's a family without you? Who will fuss at us and curse and make us get off the grass? Who will say we can't take the car? Who will promise to build a barbecue pit if you don't come?" "Well, that's different. If you all really need me, I guess I'll go. I thought you didn't want me to." "God, we'd have a dull damn house without you."

So we all prepared to move.

Now, my mother is a very efficient woman, in her mind. And

she has a lot to do. So moving day when the movers came we had only packed up the bathroom. But typical of the communal spirit, they all just packed us up and we moved.

The new house was a dream from the git. We were the first and only people to live in it. Gus planted a garden and began to fix up a den and library in the basement. Mommy had a big kitchen and a real living room. We all had a separate bedroom. It was going to be great.

I moved on down to the nursery. You were asleep so I couldn't see you and I headed back.

Yep, I would be good and glad to get home.

The nurse wheeled me down to Gary's waiting car. The nurse carried you and I carried your things. It was the first time you had on clothes and you looked really funny all dolled up and I thought: no doubt about it, the most beautiful baby in the world.

We hightailed it, though I didn't want to go quite that fast, out to Mom and Gus's. I asked Gary to slow down a couple of times but she said the air was polluted and she didn't want you exposed any more than was absolutely necessary. And I thought, that's good logic, so we hit a cruising altitude and before we knew it we were breaking like crazy for exit 19. Your sweet little hand gripped my sweaty big one and we went to sleep for the last half-mile.

When we drove up Gus ran out to grab you but Flora, Mommy's friend, was there and when he set foot in the house she grabbed you. Gary and Chris had run ahead to see if they could hold you and I struggled with your things and my things to get out of the car. Then I had to knock on the door because my hands were full and Gus said, "Come on in, Nikki. Can't I hold the baby? After all, I did name him." And I said, "Can somebody open the door?" and Chris came since he knew he was on the tail end of holding you. Then Flora, who is definitely noted for being proper and Christian and ladylike, said, "I have the baby, Gus, so you may as well go sit down because I'm going to hold him," and she put a double clutch on you and I knew there was nothing I could say. I sat down to smile benevolently at you and then Mommy said,

"Why don't you go lie down?" and Gary said, "Yeah, go lie down," and Flora, who is almost always reticent, said, "You may as well go lie down because I'm holding the baby till I leave," and she drew you closer, and I decided there was nothing I could say so I went to lie down.

They had fixed up my old room and had very bright colors on the bed and all kinds of jingle toys for you. They had bought a bassinet, which was of course blue with white lace, and three pairs of jeans. Chris later told me that was his idea since he knew little boys preferred jeans to most other clothes. I felt relatively secure when I lay down because your bassinet and diapers were in my room.

Then I noticed that it was dark and no one had been back in my room for anything. Dogs! I said to myself. They have diapers out front, I'll bet cha. So I struggled into a robe and hobbled outside. "Hi, lady," Gary said. "What cha doing outa bed?" "Yeah, Nikki, go on back to bed," Gus said. "We got everything under control." "Nik, can I hold the baby?" Chris asked and Mommy said, "Would you like a beer? I drank a lot of beer when I had Gary." So I decided to go back to bed.

The next couple of days I spent just getting oriented to being in someone else's home after having had my own for so long. Then I made the grand discovery. THE GRAND DISCOVERY. *Finnegan's Wake* is true. You have got to overthrow your parents but good or you'll live to regret it. Which is not that some parents aren't hip. Or nice. Or loving. But no matter how old you are or what you do you're a baby to your parents. I'll bet you even when Candy Stripe, the famous strip-tease dancer, goes home she's a baby to her mother. My grandmother wouldn't give my mother a key to the house when we visited her and I was old enough to remember that! Even Agnew's mother probably thinks he's still a child. If he ever was. Parents are just like that. So I decided I would have to take complete control of you if I was ever going to get back to my own house again.

First the bath. "Mommy, I think I'll bathe the baby today." "I

can do it. I took off from work so I could look after you two."
"Yeah, but they taught me a new way to bathe him in the hospital.
And you probably aren't familiar with that."

She ambled rather hysterically over to the phone to call Gary.
"I think she's still under the anaesthesia because she said I don't
know how to wash the baby," and Gary said something and she
hung up and called Gus. "I don't know who she thinks bathed her
all that time," and Gus said something and she hung up and said,
"Why don't you bathe the baby and I'll just watch?" I smiled a
sly, sly smile and thought, hurrah for me! But it wore me out so I
went back to bed while Gram got to play with a clean baby.

Tuesday after the bath, I sat down with my mother, whom we
should hereafter refer to as Gram, for a cup of coffee. "Nikki,"
she said slowly, like she always does when she has true information
to impart, "I don't want you to think I'm meddling in your business.
I know you're grown and able to take care of yourself. But don't
you think it's time you learned to bake? I didn't learn to bake until
after you were born and it's a terrible burden on your child when
everyone else has cakes and cookies homemade and your child is
the only one with sweets from the bakery."

I immediately understood the importance of what she was saying. It's true, I thought, only I remembered what it was like having
her make lumpy cakes with soggy icing. Maybe she, being a grandmother and all, could help out now. I didn't know a single grandmother who couldn't bake. And after all, who was I to scorn her offer? We younger people should recognize that the older generation
didn't survive all these years without some knowledge. So I got up
to face the blackberries. Then I understood her sneaky grandmother psychology. If I baked the cobbler I would be too tired to
feed the baby. The hurrieder I went the behinder I got and I accepted my defeat for the day.

By Wednesday I was worn out. She had won. They—because
Gus was definitely a part of it all—started coming in in the morning to get you and I would see you at lunch; then I had to go back

to bed and wouldn't see you until it was your bedtime. I somehow felt neglected. Now, it's true that I was tired and it's true that they loved me but I sat all day in my old bedroom and I couldn't play with you and I failed to see going through all that mothers go through to have grandparents take over. I decided I would have to go against my history and my ancestors' way of doing things: "I WANT MY BABY NOW, DO YOU HEAR ME? NOW!" And Gus came in to say I'd wake you up if I kept up that noise. "IF I DON'T GET MY BABY RIGHT AWAY I WILL ROUSE THIS WHOLE NEIGHBORHOOD AGAINST YOU TWO GRANDPARENTS, DO YOU HEAR ME?" And Gus told Mommy maybe they'd better bring you to me and Mommy said real low, "Or put Nikki in the basement," and I sprang at her: "AHA! I KNOW YOUR SNEAKY PLANS. ALL YOU CARE ABOUT IS TOMMY AND I WON'T STAND FOR THAT. I'M YOUR BABY AND DON'T YOU FORGET IT." Then she cuddled me on her lap and said real soothing things and walked me back to my room. I had almost gotten you and I would be more successful at dinner, I vowed. Then I had to admit that they still loved me and that did make it a lot better. Or harder. But anyway, I needed a lot of love and that's what I knew.

Friday I went back to the hospital. I was doing fine. I could go home next week and you could too. They gave me a prescription for something and I asked Gus if he'd stop on the way home and get it filled. "Gary can do it. We'd better get the boy home," he said, and I said all right. Then I realized Gary didn't know what it was and I couldn't get it until she and Chris and A. J. came out, but I thought that'll be all right, so we went on home. Then when Gary came out she took pictures of you and I took pictures of you and Gary and I forgot about it. The next morning I asked again and Gus said, "What's the rush? You'll be here another week or so." And I said, "I'll be here longer than that if I don't get it filled." And he said, "Well, there's always plenty to eat in this house and you know you're welcome to stay," and I dug it. So I said, "Tommy needs alcohol, and while you're there get this filled," and he said, "Why didn't you tell me the boy needed something?" and he flew.

I called New York and said Sunday I'd be home. Because I had to come to grips with a very important thing—as I said, *Finnegan's Wake* is true.

So everyone began adjusting to the fact that we were leaving. Mommy said, "I'll be glad because I have things to do and I haven't been doing them. Besides, I'm a busy woman and I work and I have a lot to do and won't hardly miss you at all. You know I'm a supervisor and I'm. . . ." And I said, "We'll be back Christmas," and she felt better. Gus said, "Well, it's good that you're going, Nikki, 'cause the boy cries in the middle of the night and sometimes when the ball game is on I can't even hear it, and your mother and I kinda like the peace and quiet when nobody is around," and I said, "We'll be coming in on the twenty-first so you'll have to meet us." And Gary just cried and cried and Chris said, "You shouldn't leave—you should stay and Mommy will go get your things and I'll teach Tommy how to swim," and I said, "You can come visit us, Chris, as soon as school is out and we'll be home for Christmas." And we began packing and piling into the car and Gus said he wanted to go to the airport but it was going to be frost tomorrow so he had better look after the tomato plants and everybody else just openly cried all the way to the airport but you just peacefully slept while the plane took off and we came home.

6

It's a Case of...

THE CASE OF Angela Yvonne Davis is so close to me—closer than I maybe would care to admit. But lately I have become completely secure in who I am and what that who means and have decided that neither those who love nor those who hate me can define it for me. And I will continue to love and not love those of my choosing. And I fell completely and absolutely in love with the image and idea of an Angela Yvonne, though I never have met her and now probably never shall unless we somehow end in the same camp—or prison, if you don't want to deal with camp.

I remember my first, only, last and evermore trip to California. Because of the fear I had over Colorado that some redneck would come out of the Grand Canyon, a wad of tobacco in his cheek, with his trusty bowie knife and carve the plane from the sky; because of the anticipation of seeing clusters of native Americans riding the plains after the buffalo; because of the image in my mind of the little-engine-that-could huffing across the landscape and the Black and Yellow backs that made that possible, I hated the West. I probably would have hated it if Nixon hadn't been president; I probably would have hated it if Reagan hadn't been governor; I probably would have hated it if it hadn't been winter and giving off the kind of chill that has no relationship to weather. But these things being true, I told Jesus and my juju (to be absolutely on the safe side) that if I got out of California alive, I would never return unless I had a personal message from a burning building. I transferred planes and went on to visit friends in Fresno who were going to show me California.

I couldn't deal with being shown. I just wanted to read my poetry and get out. But I stayed and we started up the coast. "Would you like to meet Angela Davis?" one of them asked and I wanted to know, "Do you know her?" He looked at me in that way a man does when you say something foolish—"I've met her," he said. And I was thinking, if I can leave tomorrow I can get back to Cincinnati, pick up my son and go on to New York, where buildings are piled on each other as they should be; back to civilization, where the air isn't fit to breathe but where one doesn't feel the necessity for carrying a gun, at least above the Delaware Memorial Bridge or maybe just at least where there is asphalt beneath your feet, or whatever rationalization I had. I didn't want to stay just to see some controversial woman—I could check a mirror or my roommate or half the people I know for that. "No, thanks, not this time. Maybe she'll come to New York." And I split, literally. The plane landed in Love Field in Dallas, Texas, and a chill so deep it could have been a beginning orgasm hit me. And I swore, as I closed my eyes to avoid seeing death walk into the plane and touch me from the storm we were flying through, that if I made it alive I would never travel beyond the Mississippi again.

I can deal with the South because I love it. And it's the love of someone who's lived there, who was born there, who lost her cherry there and loved the land—but California? Seeing those whites without the familiar streams and woods, without the familiar dirt roads? Seeing those horrendous whites with all the asphalt and light? My God! A Mississippian on a freeway! I was not prepared to deal. And Love Field should have its name changed. Should maybe be salted over, as should all of Texas—perhaps most of middle America. Terrible vibrations. And we crossed Missouri and Illinois and Indiana and I could breathe again. It was ten or eleven below when we landed in the Greater Cincinnati airport but I was warm again. I mentioned to my mother and sister I could have met Angela Davis and Mommy said, "Why didn't you, Idiot? I think she's on the ball," or something very similar, since mothers are always trying to keep up with the language but usually never quite making it. And Gary, in her informed sort of way, asked, "Who's she?" "Some Communist teacher in California. They say she's brilliant." And Gary, being extremely parochial, said, "She can't be much. I never heard of her." Then the game was on because Mommy likes to keep one up on Gary, whose frame of reference is, "Is she a friend of yours? A friend of a friend's? Then why bother?" So I missed Angela Yvonne and came on to New York and thought little more of it till summer.

I wanted Tommy to be away from these confining shores, not to mention my own needs to be if not free at least more relaxed, so we set out for Haiti in August for sunshine and Black people. Haiti was an awful disappointment. And that's an understatement. I didn't see any more poverty there than I see in Harlem and a lot less than I see in Ruleville, Mississippi. The housing was no more nor much less substandard than in many Northern communities. The health of the people seemed good and there was great love for Duvalier. The people of Port-au-Prince are an urban people, and that is a fact but an ugly one. If I had wanted Boston I could have stayed home. And the games are old ones I rejected in my youth. There is a Puritan attitude I was wholly unready for. And there was the massive game of if you're not Haitian you're foreign and therefore fair prey. I didn't want to feel like a foreigner in Haiti. I wanted to be at home with the brothers and sisters. The island, like New York, had electric generator trouble but they could have left the air-conditioning off and let us deal with the heat. The flickering lights all over the city made me very sad because it seemed the people didn't know what they had and were trying to offer what any European country would offer— only I didn't want to go to a European country. And we could not get around. I would imagine it's wholly possible if you know someone and if you speak the language but I had neither advantage. I wanted to walk the marketplace and see the island but you couldn't walk anywhere because of the unwritten law that tourists must take cabs and the cabbie is your guide, like it or not. We asked to be taken to a Haitian restaurant and the guide took us to a very bad Western restaurant, and when I said, "Well, take us where you eat," he said, "I eat here," but he didn't, and that made me angry because he could have said just no. We ordered lunch anyway and then he said he'd be back in half an hour and we gulped the food and left. We were going to walk the market-place. We found a darling little ten- or twelve-year-old and asked him to show us the market. "Just stay with me and keep an eye on your purse," he instructed, and baby on my back, I set out.

The market is beautiful: dirty as are all markets from Philly's old market to 110th Street's in New York to Knoxville's new one, but the people were great. The women laughed and pointed at how I held my baby. They would smile at me and I at them. I began to rewarm. The beggars came, pointing to obviously healthy babies to indicate hunger, and I chucked them under the chin and smiled at their mothers. Begging is probably the oldest profession in the world. A good beggar can make more than a good pro-fessional anything else. Begging in my mind is a male profession and women aren't as convincing at it as men. Prostitution, its com-petitor for longevity, is essentially its female counterpart though where white men have gone they have carried male prostitution with them. Signs of it are coming out in the islands as they are in the States and probably it is on the rise in Africa. I have respect

for beggars so that didn't color my picture of Haiti either. I'm
essentially a hustler because I'm essentially Black American and
that carries essentially a hustling mentality (if you can essentially
follow that).

As we were crossing the street with our little guide, so earnestly
and happily going about his task, a man called him aside and said
the police were looking for him. I asked why. "Your driver says I
stole you from him." And I thought, that's odd since I don't belong
to him; and I felt uncomfortable. A long discussion ensued and
then we were on our way through the market again. And I saw
the statues being turned out in the mahogany factory and I saw
the pictures that look as though they're almost all painted the same
day, and I thought, no—no, not Haiti. It's the oldest free Black
country in the Western Hemisphere. Not Toussaint's Haiti. So I
decided I'd visit the Citadel.

One of the main reasons anyone would visit Haiti is to see the
magnificent Citadel. Thousands of men walked to their deaths over
the top. This was where the island was defended. This is, if I may,
the Statue of Liberty to Haitians or at least Black people or at
least me. So I inquired. You would have thought I was asking the
Virgin Mary to see her pussy. People got secretive and protective
as if one lone Black woman could somehow destroy what the
French, Spanish and American crackers could not. Finally I pinned
the young mulatto (yes, they really are into that still) down on
when I could go and how much it would cost. "One hundred and
fifty dollars! It didn't cost that to come here." And the plane only left
every Monday and Wednesday so you had to stay overnight. I
decided I'd drive . . . only to learn you must get (1) a driver, as the
roads are extremely unreliable even in the city, and (2) passes
from each district you must go through. I decided to leave. I asked
to call the airport for a plane schedule only to be told the phones
weren't working. Then when I pulled my ugly American thing I
was told the airline ticket office was closed and you couldn't catch
a plane unless you had a reservation twenty-four hours in advance.

Haitian rum is not among my favorites and I hadn't had a serious drink since I'd been kicked out of college for a semester's binge, but I gave in. While sitting on the veranda I met two ladies from Saint Thomas who were or looked very depressed. "You need a man in Haiti," and that simple statement helped me understand that indeed I was not in a Western country and perhaps I should check myself. Tommy is very masculine and everyone was very kind to him, but he was not a man. Manly—*oui*; man—*non*. I decided to push on to Barbados, which I know and love.

The water was so clear in Barbados that I could stand waist deep and see my funny flat toes. Diamonds sparkled in the sand. The faces—the beautiful Bajans. I almost forgot Rap Brown was missing. I almost put aside Featherstone and Che. I read no papers and knew of no other tragedies. "Why do you change so," I asked a Bajan friend, "when you come to the States?" "Change?" he asked. "Yes. You come like immigrants and the first word you learn is *nigger*." "That's not true," he protested. "Why, we go to get ahead so that we can come back and live well." "But you have everything here. You can walk the beaches naked and not only will you not be molested but you won't catch any germs." "Yes, but we want to get ahead. We want to develop." "Develop to what? Air pollution. You'll soon have that with the U.S. Air Force building a base here. Policemen carrying guns. You'll soon have that with all the crazy young whites coming here." "Ah, but you mean Americans. The Canadians are nice, and the British." "To me they are all white." "Ah, but no. The Americans are terrible but the others are nice. We wouldn't be here if it weren't for the British." "But that's not true," I protested, and we walked on down the beach and soon forgot the discussion.

Probably one of the reasons I love Barbados is that I don't swim. All my life I've had a terrible fear of drowning, especially since I read *Titanic*, about a girl who dreamed of drowning and eventually wound up on the *Titanic* and met her death. I never go in more water than I can comfortably sit down in. I never go in boats of any kind and always spill gin before boarding a plane which will fly over water. But Barbados has the most gentle water in the world and I can go all the way out to where it touches my chin and I dream I'm an Olympic wave-jumper. The announcer is saying, "Now watch Giovanni take this big boy. Is she going to move? No! No! It looks like—yes! She's still standing, she's still standing!" And on the shore they are cheering wildly and I am saying, "I try to move with the wave. I try not to fight it. Now, please excuse me. I've been out there fifty-two hours setting a new record." And I smile beautifully and move through the hands reaching to congratulate me. But that morning I thought of the enigma of West Indians in the United States. They are immigrants no matter what my friend said. And they seem to feel somehow they are more American as they mistreat me. West Indians who own slums in Brooklyn and Harlem are as bad as Jewish slumlords or maybe worse because no one expects his own people to mistreat him and because they pattern themselves after absentee landlords. West Indians holding sensitive jobs that could be of some benefit to Black people always feel extremely loyal to the whites who hire them, and worse—they feel they must somehow protect the system from my insolent and arrogant indifference. They are prone to run the-little-Jew-storeowner game on you, and if you had any initiative, you would own perhaps a store. In a Jewish neighborhood? West Indians can get loans and are supported more than I by the system, and the reason is that the system will do anything to keep them in the States, holding on to their dream of their island, using them to let me know nothing is lower on earth than Black Americans. That's why Poitier could win an Oscar while Jimmy Edwards could not. That's why the great Black movie stars who are making headway are West Indian—Calvin Lockhart, for instance, though not Dick Williams. We Black Americans become resentful of this because we have worked hard and have long thought internationally only to come now to the position that parochialism is nationalism, which is internationalism. We have come now to saying that he who marches should benefit; we have come back to the concept that he who lives in the neighborhood knows that neighborhood, so that before you can organize in it you must ask the people if you are welcome. We have finally—after white folks, responsible Negroes and militants have decried the gang system—come to realize it's our strongest trump. If you're about the world nothing will get done. And we look with a jaundiced eye at those who say we must fight a war in the Congo but not in Mississippi. We worry about the voices that say we must learn Swahili but not necessarily talk to our neighbor who's crying across the room or next door. We are learning not to listen to those who focus on issues and answers in faraway lands while we are still not together among ourselves. We see riots as community control and looting as organization because we recognize that when a people or more specifically when Black people have what they want in terms of televisions and clothes, they/we still have a problem with white people: a basic disagreement concerning life styles.

I bobbed up and down in the water and thought about how beautiful a people is at home. I would have hated West Indians had I not visited Barbados. I fully understood and agreed with Harold Cruse about that. (And the issue isn't which whites are better—there is no appreciable difference between Canadians, Britishers and Americans. They are all whites, period.) While everyone in the universe feels free to fault Black Americans for being uninterested in improving relationships with brothers and sisters around the world, no one has told the brothers and sisters how to treat us. I have learned not to trust the Black immigrants but to look to the people at home before making a judgment. And I would say to West Indians and Africans, you must realize we are still at the bottom of the heap in our native country, and before you let them ship you up from your island (thereby keeping it cool and safe for them to play in) think about us here. Before you accept a job here think too about the Black people who need and deserve that job. And we will try to think about you. Many of us who would like to have not moved to the islands or Africa for that very reason. We don't want to become colonialists. We recognize that if we are serious about nationalism then we must be serious about Black people. It's arrogant of Black Americans and Africans and West Indians to think they know more than the people who inhabit another land. Which is not to say we cannot draw inspiration from each other and not at all to say one cannot make suggestions to another. But on a group scale we have seen Ghanaian resentment of Black Americans, Black American resentment of West Indians, and Lord knows which Black group West Indians hate. The playing off of Black against Black is as divisive as "Help a junkie bust a pusher." We must learn to respect each other, our men and women, our customs and habits. It will not be easy or happen overnight but it must be started. I'd like to live in Barbados, where the police not only don't carry guns but can't even ticket you—they must request that you come to court. I'd like to rear my child in clean air and fresh waters in a land not plagued by starvation and sexual hangups. But the price for that is the displacement of a Bajan. And I have learned and know that I will be easier for the government to deal with than natives as they are easier to deal with here than we are. As a nationalist I am not prepared to be anti-nationalist in my actions. And the sun kissed the water and the warmth carried over to me. I hope I can love you as I would like someday, I said to the beach as I prepared to go home.

Arriving on the West Side of New York and seeing that it was still standing, I checked my phone messages. I picked out "Your mother." And I thought, odd, since she sort of believes the phone is a wonderful, newfangled radio on which you can dial the right combination of numbers and letters and somehow a friend's voice will be there. When my sister and I were home we always did the dialing, then called her to the phone, and she still to this very day thinks we know magic. I dialed with authority and control directly.

"What's up? Somebody sick?" "No. They got your girl!" "What girl?" "Angela Davis." Damn, I thought, so it's really gonna start. "What happened?" And she ran it down. "But if they filmed it and she wasn't there I don't understand the charges." "Well, in California, if you're an accessory before the fact, they can hold you equally guilty." "That is some shit. That's like saying if you ever smiled at a Black man and that smile caused him to realize the infrequency of happiness in his life and incited him to act out his unhappiness, you are therefore guilty of rioting." "You're a writer." "Now, what does that mean?" "You're trying to be logical about white folks again." "Watch your tongue, woman. Next thing I know you'll be hopping in bed with that man you're in love with." "If you mean your father, my dear, I do already. And I'm going to hang up if you're going to be disrespectful." And I had a problem. The two Black people on the ten-most-wanted list in 1971 were/are political prisoners. And I began to think of the reality and try to compress the reality I saw as Angela Yvonne Davis. I had read Richard Wright's story "Bright and Morning Star," and while I identified with the mother I failed to understand why they latched on to communism. Then I got older and recognized that a drowning man will grab a twig. But slowly and deliberately the people were turned against the idea of communism while the two governments came closer together in policy, while Black people and white people split again—because it's been proven over and over from the beginning that white people are white first, people second, and interested in *their* white welfare third. The Communist cause, however, had a certain romance about it and a certain hopelessness that my basic Blackness made me sympathize with. And reading the transcript of the army-McCarthy hearings made me feel, why, of course those people have a right to live! They want a better life for us all. And I even got indignant that the government would try to stop it. But Russian history taught me Russia has always been an ally of the West, including the United States. And a sketchy reading of Chinese history taught me that China has always been outside. Both Russia and the United States have more fear of China than of each other.

Because Angela said she was a Communist they accuse her of being controlled or influenced by Russia. But if that were the case, why didn't she go to Russia? Why didn't the Soviet government protect her? It has a network to handle that. Why didn't the Russian Embassy offer her asylum if she was fighting the Kremlin's cause? Because clearly she was not. International communism is insidious in its moves to compromise Black people. Gus Hall and all his cohorts will say she's a party member, but how come she's the only one wanted by the FBI? If they were just looking for Communists, they could have gone to the State Department or to the Pentagon or to the CIA. If they were just looking for Communists, they could have gone to the faculty of Harvard or Princeton or any division of the University of California since the overwhelming majority of intellectuals over forty-five were at some point either members of the Communist Party or sympathizers. We've watched the Communist movement father and control the now established and reactionary labor movement. Any group that could be in any way responsible for organized labor is no threat to capitalism. We've watched the organized labor movement support Reagan and Nixon and George Wallace. We've watched Shanker encourage his union members not to teach Black children because their Black parents want control of their Black education. And we've looked with utter disgust at Bayard Rustin marching like the fool he is alleged to be, with Shanker—a lackey of his own destruction for some ideology—when clearly DuBois was right: the problem is the color line.

The world does not move on ideologies; it moves not even on interests, because it would be to the interest of some whites to unite with us. It moves on color. And that must be understood. Angela Yvonne is wanted and may be destroyed because she is Black. Her capture and destruction serve two purposes—to show Black people, most especially the middle class, what will happen if they step out of line; and to raise again the very safe and mean-ingless banner of the Red scare. Black people, which is to say colored peoples here in the United States, are backing off the Angela Yvonne Davis case, saying let the Communists defend her. But she needs our defense because she involved herself in Black action. This is the tragedy, this is the national shame of Black people. If you move to Black rhythms even your own people will turn against you. Jonathan Jackson and his friends took Black action, and white folks said at that van, no matter how many of us must die we will not let you be successful. Angela Davis was sought because as long as she was on the run, we were success-ful. The reason is not ideology. We don't even know her in-volvement with the Communists. But that doesn't matter any more than it matters whether Martin Luther King was screw-ing another woman because the question put upon us is, are we real or unreal? And we must deliver the answer. We have watched with concern the number of accidents, drug overdoses, and incidents of arrest and harassment over the past ten years, starting with the assassination of Lumumba and going to the over-throw of Sukarno and Nkrumah, the accident of Otis Redding, the prolonged illnesses of Sylvester Stewart and Aretha Franklin, the deaths of Nasser and Jimi Hendricks, the "justifiable" homicides of Sam Cooke and the Jackson State students and the blatant verbal attacks by Agnew on the public media. We have watched with con-cern the unemployment of Muhammed Ali and the slowing work schedule of Miriam Makeba and Nina Simone, as well as the sub-poena of *New York Times* reporter Earl Caldwell for refusal to divulge his sources on a Black Panther story. We feel that these and numerous unlisted complaints, such as the fact that most public and private telephones in the country are tapped and that during "emergency" periods certain people cannot either call out or receive calls, is a part if not an incitement of the present hope-lessness and fear that pervade this nation and therefore this world.

We watched Angela's face as she stepped from the motel. And

she had one of those yes-I-know looks on her face as if to say, this too must be gotten through; and as if life, which I think she values, is all that's left and she must hold on to it. And we feel this is a clear violation of her right to her opinion. All you people who said, "Bring the oppression on down," where are you? It can't get much higher. And all you people who wanted her to shoot it out with the police ought to quit watching TV. It's affecting your minds, in a dangerous way. And all you people who just wish Angela Yvonne Davis had never existed ought to be glad she does —Black, brilliant and therefore beautiful—because your turn is coming next. That's a mean sort of truth no one wants to grapple with. We keep looking for the music to stop and the lights to go out and the White House to crumble and a big sign to be put in Times Square saying, "America has fallen" or maybe "Will the real Revolution please stand?" We've watched them attempt to emasculate Huey Newton since there is no revolutionary who doesn't want children. And we ought to check ourselves when we say we want more from people who have already given all. Betty Shabazz probably doesn't sleep at night, and whether she gets a blond wig and marries a white man in no way alters the fact that Malcolm's blood runs through her daughters' veins and that he was with her. Coretta King cannot negate Martin and Jackie cannot change what John Kennedy meant. They should all in some way be unbalanced. We make jokes and say, "Wonder why she did that?" without realizing the horror of sitting with the brains of someone you loved or wanted or had in your lap; without ever dealing with the pain of sitting the children down, saying, "Be quiet, Daddy's gonna speak in a moment," and seeing thirty-eight bullets pumped into him; without ever realizing maybe they'd had a quarrel and he said, "I'll talk to you when I get back from Memphis," and he never returned and the last words he heard from you were not so soft. There is a reality to the unbalance, and we're fools if we expect anything near the normal to come out of them—if there is such a thing as normal in an abnormal world run by subnormal people.

People keep expecting Angela to be logical. But that's a twenty-six-year-old woman who probably had every reason to feel she could flow through life, find something/someone and be brainy and cute and who suddenly found herself the most wanted woman in the world. Would you come to Harlem if you were on the run? It's easy to say yes, but where in Harlem? Could she stay at the Theresa Hotel? Or maybe the hole that will be an office building? And it's easy to ask, why didn't she leave the country? But when's the last time you left? You're in danger too, and where can you go? Trotsky's enemies got him. Angela's enemies were going to get her. Probably the only person prepared to deal was not allowed out of his hotel room, was allowed no visitors, no press conference, nor a trip to Harlem because the U.S. Government was concerned for his safety. Which is probably its way of saying, "If you see Black people we'll have to kill you." And he did not see Black people. The issue of Angela Yvonne is clear. She's not an enigma; she's a young Black woman who has been thrown in with sadistic dykes, not to make sure that her spirit is broken—it was broken when they turned her in—but to show us all that our spirit can be broken. I am hoping it will have an equal and opposite effect. It will, if we follow natural laws.

The state of the world we live in is so depressing. And this is not because of the reality of the men who run it but because it just doesn't have to be that way. The possibilities of life are so great and beautiful that to see less wears the spirit down. It's like the more you move toward the possible, the more bitter you become of the stumbling blocks. I can really understand why people don't try to do anything. It's not really easy, but if you have to deal with energy it's a much more realistic task to decide not to feel than to feel. It takes the same amount of time but not to feel is ultimately more rewarding because things always come back to that anyway....

You were a fool.

The more you love someone the more he wants from you and the less you have to give since you've already given him your love. And he says, "Prove it," with the same arrogance we show when we say, "Be Black." That's a given. If I say, "I love you," don't ask how I know—move on it. Nina Simone once told me that adulthood for her would be moving on what she knows to be true. Yet to move on the ultimate truth is to sit on the corner and tell lies and bang somebody every now and then, but not too good too often because you won't be able to get rid of him. The truth is that there is this shell all around you, and the more you say, "All right, you can come in" to someone, the more he questions the right of the shell to exist. And if you fall for that and take it away, he looks at your nakedness and calls you a whore. It's an awful thing when all you wanted was to laugh and run and touch and make love and really not give a damn. Aretha said at her Lincoln Center concert, "Tell yourself everything's gonna be/ Allllllllllllllllll right." Sometimes I think the people who walk the streets in their orange pants and striped green shirts, with their Afro wigs and miniskirts, know something so deep the language hasn't been invented to express it. They know more than my political analyzing, more than the Jewish slumlord who collects the rent, more than the white men running the country and the world, more than the ritual and the Koran, more than James Brown or Roberta Flack, more than I know about who's sleeping in my bed, more than my mother knows about me and I her, more than mathematics and the little green apples and all that, because some of the infrequent times when I sit down alone I feel it too and know that that feeling is real. The Bible puts it another way: ". . . as it was in the beginning, is now and ever shall be."

7

A Spiritual View of Lena Horne

"It's a lonely ole world/ When you gotta face it/ All alone."

YOU START OUT SOMEWHERE, try Brooklyn, as a child—if you're lucky as an innocent child, if not, as a child anyway. Usually Mother and Father and other spiritual ancestors are with you—giving, taking, loving—just a little bit. With proper upbringing and proper care you too could have become an Early American; with impropriety you might have become a Cotton Club girl with a voice somewhere deep inside and *they,* hearing the rumblings of your spirit, call you a singer because *they* have never understood true rhythm. *They* called you pretty. Being pretty has always had drawbacks for Black women; being beautiful is our natural state. *They* knew you had something and *they* couldn't get it—so *they* sought control. And sometimes your life maybe looks like a box-car of the Scottsboro variety where you sat in a corner and watched the scenes—maybe Georgia was one of them where you were happy, because your feet were in red clay and you, being part Indian and part Senegalese, were at home with your family.

*From "Lonely World Blues" as sung by Amanda Ambrose.

I say it's a lonely ole world when something needs to be done and you want to do it, only no one tells you what it is. Be a cymbal for our people? Yeah, sing the funeral ditties about happiness being a thing called Joe. Ain't *they* never gonna recognize that *thing* is a five-letter word starting with p——? Or maybe it's up to us and Joe anyway. Ole Black and otherwise, maybe it's really up to us to declare him a man—*they* think men are fruits hanging from trees. Remember Billie singing about it? Lillian Smith wrote a novel about it and then resigned from CORE because she couldn't really face the problem; then she died. Or was it the other way around?

Blues is a phenomenon I once heard when Lena Horne sang "Polkadots and Moonbeams." I was in bed (children being neither seen nor heard after nine o'clock) when the voice came through the television to my antenna. And it sounded as if she meant it, which made me, even in a pre-Black stage, very sad. People aren't supposed to be mean—they can act mean; maybe they have to be that way—but are not supposed to feel something.

And it's strange how things work out—"Everything you do is right/Everything I do is wrong"—because Lena Horne has been singing a long time not to have a singing voice. I mean, she has a voice—*they* don't understand the melody. It's like living in Delaware and the DuPont factory workers being on the job a decade and someone telling you they are un/ill-equipped for the job. Looks fade. Pepshowitis is easily overcome. The mind in this country is attuned to depreciation. Can't be looks that allow Lena to entertain my mother and me. The Temptations have already said, "Beauty's Only Skin Deep," and J.B. has said, "True brothers, and money won't change you," either. So there is this phenomenon called Lena Horne who has been confused by the phenomenon named Lena Horne and who will say that she can't sing. I can't dig it because I heard her at the Waldorf do "After You" (who was she singing to?). It's like Nina Simone taking the Santa Claus out of Irving Berlin; something was brought to that song. I still think Lena Horne's untouchable.

Maybe if she'd been born in India she would have been in the Untouchables quarter (they call it segregation in reverse now) and the great Bwana would have told Gunga, "That one!" And Gunga, nigger that he was, would have said, "Horne? Can I blow that Horne?" And Bwana, as played by Bob Hope in one of the *Road* shows, would smile down his nose and say, "No, *I* got the itch." Yeah, *they* made Lena's story and starred Marilyn Monroe and Tom Ewell and then redid the sucker with Jayne Mansfield (though the leading male remained the same, which should tell us something) because Hollywood doesn't want to show a Black woman sitting on Billie's bed talking all night long about this "lonely ole world/ When you gotta face it/ All alone." *They* like the quarrels of the old with the young, *they* like division for diversion, but we ain't got time. "Would like to but can't take the time. . . ." *They* like to see you hate and be hateful/hated by husband and son and *they* have no right to see this but you cannot show anyway what is not there. *They* like to see our men go show and tell every day to the garment district, automobile factories, pulpits, bandstands, everywhere really. And as we moved away from that *they* created a poverty show which is a great comedy; we're laughing ourselves to death. *They* also have a Vietnamese and Laotian theater. Same show. Call it cowboy and Indian. Call it Coney Island (hope the Indians get that also). Call it coast-to-coast rolling. It's really all about sex anyway. WANTED: A NEW DEFINITION OF GENIUS.

Innovators are the combined energies of the people. They frequently feel guilty about taking more than they give, which should not be. The innovator who isn't taking more from the people than she is giving has nothing to give. When the people stop giving, the leader is bankrupt. Many people feed into the one person who is/ becomes the personification of the people. That's what stars are all about—a collection of mass gravitation. When the moon burned out in 1947 we began looking for bright stars. One's starmanship is based upon the ability to shed light. "It's a lonely ole world."

As Lena steps before a camera and walks to the microphone she's got to know she's not alone. Not only are her ancestors there; mine are too. We are there. Hearing her sing. And it's a funny thing about loneliness. It happens because no one understands and maybe even she doesn't understand we are there. Such is the nature of leader/followership. We were and are there to watch her show *them* and we were hopeful that *they* would see. Then when *they* didn't see she probably thought we didn't see either, but we did. Big Brother and the Grateful Dead may have been there, but so was Aretha. And that's who she sings to, and to me and all the Delta ladies and Omega men. Yeah, and maybe even the partying Kappas because when she sings we sing. And it's a proven fact that if we would all sing one note together our combined energies would turn the moon back on and the Arabs, being moon people, could reclaim their land and she could reclaim herself. Which she will do in the sunlight anyway.

Beauty is a natural wonder. One rarely looks directly at the sun and even less frequently thanks it for being itself. We especially didn't when our mood was antispiritual. But a thousand cats walking in step across the Golden Gate Bridge will break it down, just as twenty-five Black people on a Mississippi plantation doing that old Gospel shuffle, singing "The Circle Will Not Be Broken," could be heard one hundred miles. A people will come into our own. And we don't say it's better for all people, just that it's better for us. We like her better because she likes her better. And we'll like her more as we like us more, relationships being crucial.

It's all so physical, Happiness once told me. AS IT WAS IN THE BE- GINNING. The combined price must be paid. IS NOW. We've got an overdue bill to future Black people. AND EVER SHALL NOT BE. "It's a lonely ole world." We've done that. Dinah Washington did that. The earth is the giver of basil, savory, sage and mostly thyme, which should go into everything we do. But Dinah called it "Bit- ter." Aretha shouldn't have to sing that song. And Lena shouldn't feel guilty because she sang in supper clubs; after all, little Tommy

Tucker did and that brother put out some heavy dues. RISE, SALLY, RISE. We have all been lions in a den of Daniels.

It's a question of perspectives. Once we thought everything had to be done yesterday; now we feel most won't get done until tomorrow. They say it's nation time. The ability to prospect old Black (similar to though not quite the same as finding a million-dollar baby in a 10-cent store), because coal is just a diamond that didn't want to go on Jackie's fingers or around Liz Taylor's throat, is crucial. It's about old friends who let you be quiet and new friends who want to hear you talk. And Lena Horne is a spiritual experience, which is "what keeps me Black and *them* white." Lena Horne plays with unicorns and probably had a satyr steal her cherry. And she probably liked it. It's a question of perspectives. The everyday grind of being on stage must be broken. The prospect of happiness without dues is like a cracker without hatred. I mean, *they* may grow bigger tomatoes but they don't taste like anything.

Lena Horne is not a chocolate Hedy Lamarr, she's a Black Lena Horne, just as Uggams isn't a brown Smothers brother. We must come into our own. And "Do you mind?" is destructive, Horne says, because people like to hurt you under the guise of honesty and honesty without love is destructive. And one feels Lena, despite the shields, despite the time, or perhaps because of the woman. One would like to hug her and make everything all right. If one had the world of time it would take. And lacking the proper mixture of necessities some smile and say, "Hey, ain't you Lena Horne?" and walk on down 57th Street, which we did once. To my car. And I waved while she walked away and thought of my grandmother, who always used to say, "Why, my Agnes looks every bit as good as Lena Horne!" and my mother, whom I love, and my father, who loves me, and my son, who gave my life meaning. And driving to Verta Mae's book party I thought: what a shit place America is.

The Weather as a Cultural Determiner

THE CULTURE OF A PEOPLE is an expression of its life style. What defines a life style and what determines it? A Black man living at the North Pole is still a Black man—with African roots, with a Black, hence African, way of looking at his life, of ordering his world, of relating his dreams, of responding to his environment. And the strangest aspect of this Black man living at the North Pole is that his children, who have never lived anywhere but the North Pole, will retain and manifest this African way. And so will their children. And so will theirs. And even on down until one would think that all things African had been bred out of them. But when someone comes along playing a conga drum it can happen that one of these descendants will fall right into the rhythm, or he will see a Black woman and find her most beautiful, or he will sit and long for the sun, or he will meditate on his life and conjure dreams a man living at the North Pole could not conceive unless at one point Africa had been in his blood. The same with white people. A white man in Africa never becomes an African. His children never become African; they are white people living in Africa. The sight of snow brings feelings of nostalgia to them.

One of the things white people say about us is that we have no ability to delay gratification. This is in my opinion not only true but good. We came from a climate that immediately gratified us, that put all the necessities of life at our fingertips: the weather was warm; food was available from the sea and the air and the land; we could sleep outside; we could, in other words, complement our environment and survive. The very color of our skins shows that; we complemented our environment, we blended with it. On the other hand, the white man could not survive outside in Europe. To be exposed to its winters would be to perish. His home was built to protect him from the cold. His eating habits were based on his ability to measure his appetite. His survival was based on his ability to measure his appetite for life. An African who had a jones about some chick could start out walking, find her, run off to the bush and be gratified. A white man had to control his sexual urge because the nearest nonrelative might have been and most likely was miles away. In the winter months he couldn't take a chance of striking out for her. He had to wait until the weather would allow him to go. That's maybe one reason incest is more prevalent among white people than Black. That's also one reason Black people marry more than one woman. If you were cooped up in a cabin/castle with two or three women and you had a poor hunting season you were in trouble. Somebody would starve.

And I mention this because white people in America still manifest that urgency about meeting necessities despite their so-called affluence: they still hoard, they still are the ants, and we are the grasshoppers. It almost appears to be genetic. A Black man today with a million dollars will spend it and have a ball. A white man will invest and save. And one will never understand why the other did as he did. The Black man sings for enjoyment; the white man creates record companies for profit. Black people are the poets, white people the publishers.

A man in a cold environment has to order his entire life. Not only does he have to plan for necessities; he has to plan for enjoyment. His pleasure must be programmed into his life as much as his work is. This is one reason white people created prostitution; they could buy and sell it; and the chick doing it had to report on time. The Black man on the other hand could take the chance of meeting someone he wanted because he could get out to see people; if he missed today he could score tomorrow. When tomorrow is going to be freezing you have to score today, and the only way to be sure of scoring is to buy it—by contract (marriage) or extra-legally. You just don't find prostitution in Africa or the West Indies aside from what white people have created. I mention this because even a white man born in South Africa whose family has been there for as long as or longer than we have been in America will manifest the same tendencies.

Let's take it another place. The Arabs created in the image of nature: their number system starts with zero and includes the ciphers 1, 2, 3, 4, 5, 6, 7, 8 and 9, which are quite simply the sun and the nine planets. Couple the sun with any of the nine planets and you find an infinite possibility. The Roman numerals on the other hand start with I and immediately are unusable because you have to go into an elaborate system to get ten. Ten in Roman numeral becomes X, an unknown. Ten in Arabic becomes 1 plus the sun. The Honorable Elijah Muhammad teaches us that the earth is ruled by twenty-three wise scientists who obtained their knowledge from Allah, the twenty-fourth. We find this in nature. There are twenty-three chromosomes in our bodies, and our sex, hence our knowledge, is determined by the twenty-fourth chromosome. But if the twenty-fourth chromosome enters our system we become mongoloids because one cannot contain God. To see God is to travel beyond our ability to articulate that knowledge.

What I am saying is that the original man, the Black man, related to nature and tried to live within it. The white man tried to fight it.

Literature is one of the tools white people have used for survival.

The major invention of the white man in literature is the novel. The Spanish exemplar of the form is *Don Quixote,* a big, clumsily written book about a dude fighting windmills for the love of some chick who didn't dig him. It deals with chivalry and knighthood and stuff. In other words it describes the standard for a life style that no Western man could afford to live. It is quite frankly foolish. But it is long enough to take a season to get through. With a big novel in the court and someone to read a couple of chapters a week winter would pass. The modern counterpart is the soap opera. You get a little each day and tune in tomorrow—in other words, you delay your gratification. Black people come from an oral tradition. We sat by the fire and told tales; we tended the flocks and rapped poems. We had a beginning and an end for we didn't know what tomorrow would bring. We were prepared to deal with the unknown. Our laws were natural laws; they were simple and straightforward. Our laws were people-directed; the only don't was, don't kill anyone unless your tribe or community was at war. Whites' laws were property-directed; they made people property even before they had us. And it makes sense. If only so much land was fertile and was only fertile for one season, the more land you had and the more people working it, the better your chances of survival. We on the other hand had plenty all around us all the time; the land was there and we never thought to stake it out because it didn't have to be worked and it bloomed all year round. The women kept the common land and the men did the hunting and fishing. All shared. Still today if you go to a Black's house, even if he has very little, he'll share and be insulted if you refuse. Those of us from the North who worked in the South during the sit-in days were constantly surprised by the people's generosity. And their generosity was based not on some moral law but on the fact that wherever you find Black people they share and say to hell with tomorrow. That isn't negative; it's based on our collective historical need. Even a dude who doesn't want to is compelled to share. Call it an irresistible impulse. White folks say we are illogical.

Logic is the spiritual understanding of the subjective situation and the physical movement necessary to place life in its natural order. In other words, on some gut level we understand that we all will survive or we all will not survive, and my hoarding a little corn or your hoarding a little meat will not let us make it. But if we get together we can have at least one good meal, which may give us the strength to push forward the next day. A Black person will have one big meal and thoroughly enjoy it even if he knows there will be nothing tomorrow. He will be full for one day. The white man will measure out and starve himself or never be full forever.

We have been called nonreaders.

Blacks as a people haven't jumped into long books because they usually have proven to be false. White people write long every-thing—novels, epic poems, laws, sociology texts, what have you—because they are trying to create a reality. They are generally try-ing to prove that something exists which doesn't exist. We rap down on a daily level because we appreciate our existence. We had many gods, one for damned near everything we could get our hands on, while they had one (how many gods could one castle hold?) who was the most together dude of all. They were waiting on a messiah to solve their problems; we had no problems to be solved. We are the poems and the lovers of poetry.

Poetry is the culture of a people. We are poets even when we don't write poems; just look at our life, our rhythms, our tender-ness, our signifying, our sermons and our songs. I could just as easily say we are all musicians. We are all preachers because we are One. And whatever the term we still are the same in the other survival/life tools. The new Black Poets, so called, are in line with this tradition. We rap a tale out, we tell it like we see it; someone jumps up maybe to challenge, to agree. We are still on the corner —no matter where we are—and the corner is in fact the fire, a gathering of the clan after the hunt. I don't think we younger poets are doing anything significantly different from what we as a people have always done. The new Black poetry is in fact just a manifestation of our collective historical needs. And we strike a responsive chord because the people will always respond to the natural things. We are like a prize stallion that Buffalo Bill thought he'd tamed. Then the free horses (they call them "wild") came by and called, and without even knowing why, we followed. And those who couldn't follow, like any caged animal, whined and moaned and then began to kick the door down. The call has been made and we are going to be free.

We don't know who our great poets are; we have no record of the African poems before we were set upon by the locusts. And like that dreaded insect they ate/destroyed everything in sight. Call them French destroyers. They started with the physical and went into the mental. I can well imagine a man sitting in a village watching the whites approach. He at first wondered what kind of insect was that large. He probably ran for the No-Roach, and then in a typical humane manner decided to wait to see if it was friendly. The insect presented itself as a man who wanted to learn. And he did. He studied at our universities; he lived in our villages. And in peace. We often make the mistake of thinking that the white man came and destroyed right away. In actuality he learned. He invited our scholars to Europe. We had an exchange. Then after he had taken, as all carbons take, the form, he began to destroy the original. But he didn't have the feeling. He didn't have the ability to create. He didn't have the essence. We spoke of personal freedom; he made it a law—with no emotional understanding of the simple fact that personal freedom cannot be made into a law. How can you order someone to be free? And even the most liberal of the countries, which was America at its inception, held it to be self-evident that all men were created equal, which meant that all men were entitled to life, liberty and the pursuit of happiness. But the earliest laws among whites were property laws, and even today the fight is still for control of land because they could not/cannot understand life and happiness aside from the ownership of real estate. And to them the realest estate has got to be the control of other men.

So we sang our songs and they copied what they could use and mass-produced it and banned what they didn't understand. We told our tales to their children and they thought we loved them. Just listen to "Rockabye Baby" and picture a Black woman singing it to a white baby—when the east wind blows the cradle will rock and down will come baby, cradle and all. Or Peter, Peter, pumpkin eater, put her in a pumpkin shell and there he kept her. They didn't know we were laughing at them, and we unfortunately were late to awaken to the fact that we can die laughing.

We have a line of strong poets. Wheatley by her life style was a strong woman intent on survival. And it's funny that all her poems talking about the good white folks are reprinted but not the poems about her hard life. I've seen only a few of her later poems and at that only once. They say her writing wasn't good after she married that Black man and had children. They say the same thing about Chesnutt. He was fine when he was publishing without anyone knowing that he was Black; after that they say his writing went down—especially in works where Black folks come out on top, like *The Marrow Tradition* and *The Wife of His Youth*. And we've got to dig on the whole scene because whites have been the keepers of records and they've only kept the ones they like. My theory is that the older we get as a people here in America the more we are going to check ourselves. There are many fine works locked away in trunks; there are many fine poems running in the heads of the old people. We should always talk with old people because they know so much. Even the jivest old person, in line with his collective historical need, can give a history of some movement or maybe just his block and the people on it. The tales that we trade on the corners are taken seriously. Lives have been lost over one version or another, and it's not because Niggers just like to kill Niggers but because we have a duty—call it a religious calling—to record and pass on orally.

Black is a sacrament. It's an outward and visible sign of an inward and spiritual grace. A poetry reading is a service. A play is a ritual. And these are the socially manifested ways we do things. There have been Black novelists, Black writers of history, Black recorders of the laws, but these are not tools for the enjoyment of the people. These are tools for the scholars. And I am not knocking them. For when Black people have been recorders we have sought truth; when white people used these tools they sought dreams.

We hear a lot about the Black aesthetic. The aesthetic is the dream a culture wishes to obtain. We look back when we seek an aesthetic; whites look forward. In my opinion the search for an aesthetic will lead down a blind alley which will have a full-length mirror on three sides and at the end—we are our aesthetic. Given the definition of aesthetic, it already is the Black life style in whiteface. What white people are seeking is the removal of the pressure of the "real" world from their backs. The word closest to that in Blackdom is bourgeoisie. And Greer and Cobb call them dilettantes—a small group not worth worrying about. Most of us accept the responsibility of/for living. It's very worrisome when we find Black people committing suicide by dope, self-hatred and the actual taking of life. It means we have gotten away from our roots. This is when the poet must call. Brothers, brothers everywhere and not a one for sale. Jewel Lattimore calls it utopia. The poet calls in *Youngblood* when big strong Joe Youngblood comes to take his wife. The poet called when Stokely said, "Black Power." The poet calls when Rap says, "Come around or we gonna burn you down." The poet called when Rosa Parks said, "no." We are our own poems. We must invent new games and teach the old people how to play. The poet sang "What happens to a dream deferred?" Or when the O'Jays summed up the sit-in movement asking, "Must I always be a stand in for love?" The poet called when Sterling Brown said, "The strong men keep coming." Or when Margaret Burroughs asked, "What shall I tell my children who are Black?" Or when David Walker addressed his *Appeal to the Colored People of the World with a Special Message for the Black People in America*. Or when LeRoi Jones said, "Up against the wall, motherfuckers." Or when the young men out of work asked, "What I wanta work for?" The poet calls with the cry of the newborn. "Get on the right track, baby."

9

The Beginning Is Zero

I'VE FINALLY LIVED long enough to realize Black people are not fools. Many things, perhaps, but not fools. That Booker T. Washington could have a dream and excite enough Blacks in it to make the bricks that built the buildings is fantastic. There are many side arguments about the value and validity of his dream but Tuskegee is alive . . . it's a Black institution. You say *Ebony* is just *Look* or *Life* in Blackface? Try telling that to Mississippians who made a best seller of *Before the Mayflower*. We know better. *Black World* has never been *Reader's Digest* and SNCC has never coordinated. What we mean is, nothing starts from one. It starts from zero. In literature Charles Chesnutt is our zero. And we swim or sink on his accomplishments.

Chesnutt's first published stories are contained in *The Conjure Woman*. He began publishing them in the *Atlantic Monthly* because they thought he was white—just as many writers are published in it now because the *Atlantic Monthly* thinks they are Black. It's a question not of passing but of posture. *The Conjure Woman* puts Joel Chandler Harris and Stephen Foster and all those dudes up to and including Styron in their places. Uncle Julius is out to win. And he does. He convinces the cracker that the grapes have a spell on them and are therefore better left alone. He shows what would happen if the white man had to live in the Black man's shoes in "Mars Jeen's Nightmare." And he keeps his nephew's job for him. He uses the white woman's natural curiosity about Black men to his advantage. She always sympathizes with him while her husband is prone to back off. He is a good Black politician. The cracker gives the lumber that is "Po' Sandy" to the Black church. Uncle Julius is one of Black literature's most exciting characters precisely because he is so definite about his aims. He intends to see his people come out on top. John, the white voice, thought he could use Julius while it was the other way around. And Chesnutt drops a few gems on us dispelling the romantic theory about slavery's charms. In "Goophered Grapevine," for example, a new slave eats the grapes and is bound by the terms of the goopher to die. "The overseer said on the first rainy day he would take the slave to see the Conjure woman." Well, if he is bound to die wouldn't it be worth taking him right away? Not if it is just a slave. And Henry is sent out and sold and resold to suit the convenience of the household with no thought of him. And Sandy of "Po' Sandy" is treated the same way. Rather than be a slave he'll be a tree and plant his roots by the river? But he is destined to be cut down anyway—unless he fights back.

Chesnutt's second collection was *The Wife of His Youth*. Charles Chesnutt was born of free parents in Cleveland, Ohio. His family was from North Carolina. Chesnutt began a saga-type tale which is still being used by novelists like Attaway and Hal Bennet and which was and is the pattern of movement of Black people— from rural South to urban North. And this was in the 1800s to early 1900s. Naming his mythical city Groveland (after Grover Cleveland perhaps) he moves his newly emancipated Black men and women along the social scale. Mr. Ryder in the title story has come

North and made his fortune in the post office. He is about to wed a lovely light-skinned young lady whom he loves when an old Black woman comes asking his help in finding her husband. He is that husband she seeks. He decides to acknowledge her, thereby giving up much he thought he wanted. Is this just a jive short story or wasn't it in fact exploring the historical relationship between Black man and Black woman when, after emancipation, he chooses to "better himself" and leave her behind? Chesnutt's main fault was perhaps his optimism. He accomplished in that story one of the goals we seek from literature—the truth and its ideal ending.

"Her Virginia Mammy" was the forerunner of that horrendous novel which was made into that equally horrendous movie, *Imitation of Life*, which had you know who crying in the aisles even after the third viewing. It's all in his story—the stereotypical self-sacrificing, self-denying mother and the child who should have a better chance. This is an important story because later his novels negate it. Who hasn't at some time thought it would be easier to be white? And how many have actually overcome that? Two of Chesnutt's best known stories, "The Sheriff's Children" and "The Web of Circumstances," both appear in *The Wife of His Youth*. Both these story themes have since resounded in white literature, from the *Ox Bow Incident* to *To Kill a Mockingbird*. Chesnutt, by making the Black man innocent and the white man his executioner, introduced Jesus as a Black man into the American context.

We can easily see that Charles Chesnutt set a tone for literature in America. What is clear is that they can praise you or damn you, but after a certain point they cannot ignore you. And we cannot ignore many people who preceded us. Surely E. Franklin Frazier was inspired in his classic study of the Black bourgeoisie by "Baxter's Procastus." Baxter, who belongs to an exclusive men's club, decides to write a book, which he then sells to all his fellow club members. They all tell him how wonderful it is and how much they enjoyed it. Then on a whim one of the newer members of the club decides to open the book. It is a sealed copy since sealed copies are more valuable than unsealed. He opens it to find all the pages blank, exposing the fact that the other members either did not or could not read. Baxter had a good laugh and the bourgeoisie suffered embarrassment. And yet they haven't learned, if a current observation is an indication. I recently attended a writer's conference where one writer began a question to another with "I haven't read your book but I understand it's salacious." That's a big word if the book wasn't read. But it's all in the story with the humor and love that only one who had been there and escaped could give.

Chesnutt's novels are deserving of much time and attention. He wrote three though I will touch on only the first two (the third is out of print)—*The Marrow of Tradition* and *The House Behind the Cedars. The House Behind the Cedars* was written first. It deals with a man who is passing for white and his sister. The brother has gone away and married well and is living a comfortable life. He comes back to the house behind the cedars to take his sister away with him. She would like to come but she really can't. She goes with her brother to live in his big house and be a part of his society; yet she is haunted by dreams of her mother and a man she has left behind. She cannot dance between the two worlds. Her roots are deep in the soil that gave her birth. When her mother needs her she tries to go home briefly, but to look back is to have the curse of Lot's wife upon you.

Chesnutt's view of the Black woman is remarkably accurate, even in the stilted language of his time. The Black woman historically has never been able collectively to move from her roots. Too many emotional strings are wound around her. It is man's place to go forth and conquer; it is woman's to seek the soft, warm places. Man expels; woman receives. Chesnutt resolved the question for all of them—from Lillian Smith to Alice Childress. There are two realities within the Black community and two within the white. One is the reality of men and the other that of women. Black men control the Black reality as white women control the white. We are what he is. Otherwise why this talk about manhood? They are what she is. Otherwise why the lynching and knighthood stuff to defend her honor? We now recognize that a bunch of misfits came to these shores to populate this nation. If white men were not successful in making those misfits into "ladies," their nation would never win the respect of the world. Look at Jackie Kennedy—a plain, ordinary, maybe even not bright white girl made out to be the epitome of grace and charm. And when she married a non-Westerner the nation went up in arms. Never mind what white men have done; it all turns on white women. That's why women in New Orleans spit on Black kids: they have a lot to protect. And before Women's Lib can convince some of us that we should be involved in the Movement, that act will have to be fully and carefully explained. Black women have always known where white society was weakest, just as whites have known that the way to keep the Black man under their thumb is to hold us down. The weight of Blackness ultimately falls on Black men. And it is their response which will determine our position. This is clearly outlined in Chesnutt's novel.

The Marrow of Tradition was the beginning of the end of white folks' love affair with Chesnutt. He checked his antecedents and thought perhaps David Walker had something in his *Appeal*. Chesnutt wrote the first race riot and the critics began grumbling that perhaps he had lost his touch. The plainer he made it the more they hated him. The old Mammy dies in the riot. The Black folks fight back. The crackers are milling around smoking their cigars, deciding which Black folks will have to die, while we are preparing for a siege. It's so real and so graphic:

> In the olden time the white South labored under the constant fear of negro insurrections. Knowing that they themselves, if in the negroes' place, would have risen in the effort to throw off the yoke, all their reiterated theories of negro subordination and inferiority could not remove the lurking fear, founded upon the obscure consciousness that the slaves ought to have risen. . . . There was never on the continent of

America, a successful slave revolt nor one which lasted more than a few hours or resulted in the loss of more than a few white lives.

—*The Marrow of Tradition*

Yet Josh and the men come to Lawyer Watson and Dr. Miller and ask them to lead. Each of the Black men has an excuse. One says it will blow over, the other that he will be killed. Josh and the men make the monumental decision that must be made by the masses when the bourgeois show their real lack of color—that they will lead themselves. They will not allow white men to continue this madness that the educated coloreds seem not to mind so much after all. Miller, the protagonist, goes off romantically looking for his wife and child. Watson flees for his life. But Josh and the men move on across town. That kind of truth in literature hadn't been done before and is rarely done now.

Chesnutt used what we now call dialect, but given our use of language it is more accurately termed slang. And since it isn't our language anyway it doesn't matter how he spells it. It is for us to define the positive in and the negative out of our literature. (Chesnutt clearly showed in his all too brief career the limits of writing Black. LeRoi Jones has come under the same pressure in the same way. Jewish critics now say Jones "can't write" as the WASP critics once said of another genius, Charles Chesnutt. Once you write for your people others will judge that your quality is failing. And we find it regrettable that Black critics don't more frequently view works from a Black perspective. A true numbers system starts with the son (sun) and that would be Charles Waddell Chesnutt..

10

Black Poems, Poseurs *and Power* °

I LIKE ALL the militant poems that tell how we're going to kick the honkie's backside and purge our new system of all honkie things like white women, TV, voting and the rest of the ugly, bad things that have been oppressing us so long. I mean, I wrote a poem asking, "Nigger, can you kill?" because to want to live under President no-Dick Nixon is certainly to become a killer. Yet in listening to Smokey and the Miracles sing their *Greatest Hits* recently, I became aware again of the revolutionary quality of "You Can Depend on Me." And if you ask, "Who's Loving You?" just because I say he's not a honkie you should still want to know if I'm well laid. There is a tendency to look at the Black experience too narrowly.

The Maulana has pointed out rather accurately that "The blues is counterrevolutionary," but Aretha is a voice of the new Black experience. It's rather obvious that while "Think" was primarily directed toward white America, Ted White could have taken a hint

°Reprinted from *Negro Digest*, vol. XVIII, no. 8, June, 1969, pp. 30–34.

from it. We must be aware of speaking on all levels. What we help to create we will not necessarily be able to control.

The rape of Newark in the 1968 election was criminal. If revolutionaries are going to involve themselves in politics, they should be successful. And while I'm sure poems are being written to explain the "success" of the Newark campaign, and essays and future speeches are being ground out on brand-new Scot tissues in living color blaming the Black community for not supporting the United Brothers, I would imagine the first problem the United Brothers encountered that they were unable to overcome is that they were not united.

LeRoi Jones, for whatever reason, had no business appearing on a show with Anthony Imperiale issuing joint statements about anything at all because he (LeRoi) did not have equal power in his half of the joint. Joint statements and meetings with the Governor did not encourage the Black people of Newark to support the United Brothers. Because of the prestige of LeRoi, no Newark voice is being lifted to analyze what went wrong. In the all-Black central ward, of the people who turned out to vote only 50 percent voted for councilmen, period. They did not vote against the United Brothers but they would not vote for them either. In a year when Black people showed little to no interest in national politics the stage was set for massive involvement in Black Power. There was no opposition—the people were not involved in another camp. So what went wrong?

Militarism, for one thing. To enter the main headquarters of the United Brothers one had to sign in. This turned most people off. Then you were asked quite tersely, "What do you want?" And if you couldn't answer concisely and accurately you were dismissed. The extreme of this behavior at headquarters was reached when a man carrying $600 to give to the campaign was requested to sign in and then engaged in conversation by one of the keepers of headquarters. The man turned from the conversation to speak with someone else and was told by a second headquarters keeper, "The brother wasn't finished with you." When the man's response wasn't satisfactory they pushed him up against the wall and the brothers "guarding" him were told, "Do anything necessary to keep him in line." The man with the money finally made his way upstairs and complained to Karenga and LeRoi. He was told his treatment was "an honest mistake."

It was a disaster. If that kind of treatment was accorded a man with as much prestige as he had, I shudder to think what happened to those who just drifted in to see. They offered an apology to the offended brother but that missed the point entirely. The people of Newark became more afraid of the Black candidates and their organization than they were of the present scandal-ridden, Black-hating administration. This is too bad—to put it mildly. The contradictions are too great.

Revolutionary politics has nothing to do with voting anyway. But if we enter electoral politics we should follow the simple formula that every Black person is a potential vote and must be welcomed and treated as such, with or without dashiki, with or without natural.

The latent militarism of the artistic community is even more despicable—art and the military have always been traditionally opposed. We saw the epitome of the new alliance at the 1968 Black Power Conference at Philadelphia. Every artist worth his salt had a military wing attached to him. The conference had guards; the artists had guards; the guards had guards even. One of the highlights of the conference to me was Karenga's guards complaining about Stanford's guards. This is foolish because it has already been proved beyond a reasonable doubt—with the murders of Martin Luther King, Jr., and Robert Kennedy—that anybody the honkie wants to take off he not only can but will, whenever and however he wants to stage it. The artist-guard syndrome seems to center around the impression we can make with the various communities. The artist impresses the white community with his militancy and the guards impress the Black community with their power. It's a sick syndrome with, again, the Black community being the loser. There is no cause for wonder that the Black community is withdrawing from involvement with the Black artist.

On "Soul," which appears on educational TV in New York, the same simplistic crap has taken place. "Soul" is funded by the Ford Foundation and the Negro Ensemble Company is funded by them also. Yet the people on "Soul," after giving Barbara Ann Teer credit for founding NEC, put it down as not being Black enough. And the Last Poets, which is probably a truer title than they know, performed *Die Nigga*. It's just not the same concept as "kill." It would seem to me that the most important and valid aspect of cultural nationalism would be the support of other Black cultural ventures, especially since one cultural function is funded by the same white folks who fund the group being put down.

Since Black people are going to look at TV they should look at "Julia." Diahann Carroll is prettier, i.e., more valid, than Doris Day any day of the year. And while the idea of cops is bad to me, period, and extralegal Black cops are even worse, if Black people are going to watch cop shows on TV then "Mod Squad" beats the other white vigilante shows. And if "I Spy" is indeed, as I've been told, the new Lone Ranger, then Bill Cosby, by becoming the new Tonto, should help make us aware that we are the Indians of this decade. The parallel institutions that we hear so much about must certainly have reached their apex with "I Spy." *For Love of Ivy* is as fine a movie as we've had since *Nothing but a Man*. And it's certainly more valid to us than *Planet of the Apes, 2001* and those other white things we are forced to watch. It would sometimes appear some elements of the Black artistic community are against popular success unless it's theirs. Sidney Poitier has moved into the area where we have said we want actors to go—only we didn't mean, and make money, I guess. Everybody knows *Guess Who's Coming to Dinner?* is a bad movie but it is neither the beginning nor the end of Poitier's career, and the righteous indignation we spout is really quite out of place. Black people will soon quit listening to us if we can't get in tune with them. I would imagine it's a question of wigs.

Everybody has done his wig poem and wig play. You know, where we put Black people down for not having taken care of business. But what we so easily forget is our own wig. While we put down commercially successful artists we scramble to the East Side to work, we fight for spots on TV, we move our plays downtown at the first chance we get—we do the very things we say are not to be done. Just because our hair is natural doesn't mean we don't have a wig. We are niggers-in-residence at white universities and talk about voting as a means to take over a city, and then we put James Brown down for supporting Hubert Humphrey. It's all a wig. We obviously have no concept of power because if we did we'd recognize that the power of Black people forced James Brown to go natural. Everybody can't come up through the civil rights movement because it just doesn't exist anymore. When Black boys and girls from Mississippi to Massachusetts write J.B. letters complaining about *This Is My Country Too* (or was that a John A. Williams book?) then we ought to rejoice that Brown changes his position. The people we purport to speak for have spoken for themselves. We should be glad.

And it's not as though—if we just like to complain—there isn't an abundance of issues to complain about. What was John Coltrane doing with music that made some people murder him? Why isn't Otis Redding's plane brought up from the lake? What about the obvious tieups in the murders of John and Robert Kennedy with Martin Luther King's death? What elements in this country conspired to murder both Richard Wright and Ben Bella? What did Malcolm and Nkrumah say to each other that caused one to die and the other to be overthrown? Why have so many Arabs and people of Arab descent been arrested for murder or conspiracy to commit murder? And I'd like to know what the cultural nationalists think about James Forman, living with a white woman who has borne his children, controlling and directing SNCC while Stokely, married to a Black woman, was kicked out. These are cultural questions—relating to survival. But it sometimes seems that the only thing that culturalists care about is assuring themselves and the various communities that they are the vanguard of the Black Revolution. They have made Black women the new Jews while they remain the same old niggers. We have got to do better than this.

Our enemy is the *New York Times,* not the *Amsterdam News;* it's *Look* and *Life,* not *Ebony;* and we ought to keep our enemy in sight. If we're going to talk about parallel institutions then we have to recognize the parallel institutions we have. It is just not possible to have a crisis in Negro intellectualism unless we recognize that Negro intellectualism exists. Young writers ought to recognize that an old writer can't put down other old writers for our benefit. It's sometimes better for a swimmer flailing around in a turbulent lake to be left to drown than for other swimmers to go under also in trying to save him. This may, however, be a personal decision.

One of the main points I'd like the culturalists to remember is that the Jews had more than 100 art festivals while in the concentration camps. The Warsaw ghetto itself became the cultural place to play until the Germans carted the inhabitants off. And while it pleases me to know that we are making cultural strides, it also worries me that we are failing to make political connections. Poems are nice, but as someone points out, "They don't shoot no bullets." "We must," as Marvin X says, "read our own poems." As a group we appear to be vying with each other for the title Brother or Sister Black. That will not get us our freedom. Poor people have always known they are Black, as Rap Brown pointed out, just as poor honkies have always known they are white. These are facts. We need to know where our community is going and to give voice to that.

The Onyx Conference in 1969 showed just how far from the community we had strayed—we didn't even want people there who weren't artists. We are in grave danger of slipping away from our roots. The new hustle, starting with Claude Brown and brought to its finest point by Eldridge Cleaver with his hustle of Huey Newton, seems to be who can get the ear of the enemy for enough money and/or prestige to float on a pink damn cloud to the concentration camps. Everyone who is breathing easy now that Wallace wasn't elected ought to check again—that's gas you're smelling, artist— and it will take more than a Black poem or your Black seed in me to rid this country of it.

11

The Sound of Soul,
by Phyll Garland: A Book Review
with a Poetic Insert

IN THE LAST DECADE perhaps the most beautiful soul sound, and certainly our choice for the number 1 all-time Black parade, is "Ain't Gonna Let Nobody Turn Me Round" as sung by Martin and the Freedom Riders, challenged only by Stokely and the Militants with their updated version of "Black Power" (the tune that made Nat, Sojourner and the Frederick—sometimes called the Black Rascals —so popular). Perhaps if negro writers (and we use the term advisedly) were more aware of soul sounds and less interested in the sound of soul there would be more clarity over what we are about. All the singers aren't on stage and few of the songs are protected by BMI.

The current run to do something Black, like eating soul food or dancing in the streets, did not create Black music. And we would think Black people, particularly here in America, will be singing those down home blues again very soon since the suburbs have pushed the price of chittlings to 40 cents a pound, greens up to two pounds for a quarter, and you can't find chicken feets at all. As

Marvin and Tammi said, "Ain't Nothing Like the Real Thing, Baby." Janis Joplin never sang the blues. And we can only consider it a sign of our own continued self-hatred for her to be thought soul. Xerox Corporation makes an excellent copy but you wouldn't want to dance to it. Sly and the Family Stone said, "Thank You Faletinme Be Mice Elf Agin." Which is very deep because they're talking to us—not them. We've always been ourselves and are always gonna be. And it's amazing to us why negroes create unnecessary conflicts for themselves, as if they don't have enough to do just being oppressed. Black people must become the critics and protectors of Black music. A people need to have something to ourselves.

There are many loose ends that could have been tied together if a little more time had been put in. Nina Simone quotes a poem at the end of her interview. The poem is "Utopia" by Jewel Lattimore, a Chicago poet who we're sure could use the publicity. There is the overlong chapter on Stax and the nonexistent one on Motown. And we never considered sister Aretha, the top soul singer of the last couple of years, a "minister's daughter from Detroit." Something more needed to be said. B. B. King, whom we remember from way back, along with Jimmy Reed, was in our opinion done a disservice by the sly hinting that Albert King, a Stax come lately, is his brother. On a trip of his to New York I visited the show he was appearing in and asked him the "delicate question" Garland didn't wish to pose. Mr. King replied, "Albert King is my brother like you are my sister." Now, that wasn't so hard to find out. I would imagine it's difficult to do a book centering on the now, as Garland—*Ebony's* New York editor—has done. Yet there are many points that we feel simply should be brought out.

When a bright teenager began hanging around Berry Gordy, sometime songwriter for Jackie Wilson, wanting to do a tune, Gordy told him to GO GRADUATE. He did, came back and made "Way Over There." And the Motown sound was on its way. Then came Diana Ross and the Supremes, the Temptations and the scores of R&B stars who brought back the sound of Harvey and the Moonglows, the Clovers, Luther Bond and the Emeralds, Hank Ballard and the Midnighters. There could be no book on R&B without Hank Ballard. He was most definitely a forerunner of James Brown, talking about a "thrill upon the hill, let's go, let's go, let's go." And how can you overlook "The way you wiggle when you walk/Could make a hound dog talk," a direct link to the old blues? Or "Annie Had a Baby, Can't Work No More"? "Work with Me, Annie" was stolen by bug-eyed Teresa Brewer, called "Dance with Me, Henry," and made lots of money for the insignificant others. Speaking of Brewer, she also stole Sam Cooke's song "You Send Me" (somebody really should have). And Dorothy Collins and "Your Hit Parade" was born. We have paid a high price for breaking into white time. I mean, Snooky Lanson? "The Bob Crosby Show" with Joanie Sommers doing "Most of All" "Sincerely." A high price.

And Garland doesn't even mention Harvey Fuqua and the Moonglows. "We Go Together." Harvey teaming with the former queen of soul, Etta James, for "My Heart Cries." (Actually the other side was the hit but that's what I dug since I'm a romantic.) Harvey now works for Motown. Etta James and Richard Berry were among the first duos to click. Mickey and Sylvia. "Come On, Baby, Let the Good Times Roll" (I've forgotten their names but never the good times). These were forerunners of Marvin and Tammi. And the teaming of the Supremes with the Temptations. If one on one was good then more should be better. And could there be an R&B book without mention of "Earth Angel"? The Penguins were the first group to be named after animals. (We even lead in that.) Or the Moroccos singing "Red Hot and Chili Mack." That's a direct link. Or making sense out of the overdone "Somewhere over the Rainbow," saying, "Pardon My Tears, Pardon My Tears." The Flamingos singing "I Only Have Eyes for You," keeping a family tradition going—the lead singer is Bill Kenny's (of the Ink Spots) son. And where, pray tell, were the Dells? They are the only group to have hits in the 1950s ("Oh, What a Night") and come back intact in the 1960s ("There Is"). That's worthy of mention. The

Chicago people were woefully neglected. Curtis Mayfield and the Impressions have been with us from "Gypsy Woman" through "We're a Winner" to "Mighty, Mighty (Spade and Whitey)," and Mayfield has other significance because of Curtom, one of the few Black record companies. His company has been instrumental in bringing younger groups along, most notably the Five Stairsteps.

I think Garland got hung up on the dream of integrating and ignored Black music for integrated music. Stax would certainly be allowed, if I ruled the world, to do what it wants, but a book on soul should deal with soul. The people who have been abused by the insignificant others are being abused by Garland also. Stax, like Motown, started in the Black community, one in a house, one in a theater. It was one man's dream, like Motown. People came in off the streets begging to be recorded, as at Motown. The main difference is that Stax started off white and Motown was Black. Now both appear to be white or extremely integrated. What happened to Motown? It's easy to see an insignificant other just plundering a good thing but Gordy knew what he was trying to do. Why didn't Garland dispel the rumors that the Mafia told Gordy he could have half of Motown or all of nothing? If the rumor is true then we can understand why Temptations puzzle people. We can understand why Florence Ballard would rather quit than fight. Why didn't Garland look into Ed Sullivan's connections with the people who rumor has it took over Motown? If Sullivan doesn't own a part of it now why didn't Garland dispel that rumor? Many important questions could have been cleared up if time had been taken.

Then there is VeeJay. Jimmy Reed recorded for VeeJay. The group that sang "Little Mama, I need your loving but I wasn't true to you" recorded with VeeJay. The Charms, among other groups, were recording with VeeJay. And it just folded—while Atlanta and its subsidiary Epic got fat off our sound. Why? And why did they all of a sudden just close Blue Note and auction everything in the building off? Why is Motown suing T-Neck and the judge (à la the Dred Scott decision) say, not only am I ruling against you but every other judge will too? That sounds a little out of order. Reminds us of the automobile accident the Impressions' band had where two members of the band were killed. Before verification could be made they were doing eulogies of the Impressions. (Could that have been the inspiration behind "Choice of Colors"?) And what happened to Volt? It used to be Stax-Volt (which despite the length of time spent on Stax Garland fails to mention). Redding's brother, probably because he was grief-stricken, accused certain insignificant others of Italian origin of murdering his brother. Of course some do consider it strange that the plane has never been exhumed. And that the radar was exactly three miles off (which put the plane in the lake rather than the airport). To say something about Redding and not mention the Voter Registration project he was doing in Macon is to do his memory a disservice. Not to mention the youngsters he was sending to school is to overlook a great part of his soul. And why was there no chapter or paragraph or even a tiny sentence on Macon? Redding, James Brown and Little Richard, to name the giants, are all from Macon. That town must put out some heavy blues.

The blues didn't start with Dixieland or work songs or Gospel or anything but us. It's really catering to insignificant others to try to delineate our music. The cadences heard in bolero are heard in the jungle, and we all know the Philadelphia Philharmonic hasn't yet appeared in the Congo. (That's what the war is all about!) Dvořák's "Fifth," commonly called "The New World Symphony," is nothing but our music, which Garland mentions. But she fails to mention that the "Fifth" is done but not Mingus' "Freedom Suite." She correctly calls "classical" music formal music but she doesn't state that it is formally Black. All music in the world is Black music. Or was until it was imported and, like good dough in the hands of a bad cook, kneaded and bent until it was too tough for us to handle. The blues haven't been reborn because they have never died. But the blues, like the sermons, like the colloquialisms that mark our speech, have always been just beyond the grasp of the insignificant others. The blues today are sung by Leon Thomas to Pharaoh's horn, are created in drum suites by Milford Graves, were constantly with Coltrane, and Shep sleeps with them probably every night. The blues were never popular as we deal with the mass media. Negroes were ashamed of them, didn't understand them, just as they don't understand Ornette, Don Pullen, the Aylers. And when Jerry Wexler or the unholy Stax finally learns a way to package it we will be off into something else. A people need to have something all to ourselves. The blues will be with us until we are free.

Garland, we think properly, gave the history of Black music over to LeRoi Jones. But the field she opted for herself is still largely untouched. Nobody deals with Aretha, a mother with four children, having to hit the road. They always say, "After she comes home." But nobody ever says what it's like to get on a plane for a three-week tour. The elation of the first couple of audiences, the good feeling of exchange. The running on the high you get for singing good and loud and long, telling the world what's on your mind. Then comes the eighth show on the sixth day. The beginning to smell like the airplane or bus. The if-you-forget-your-toothbrush-in-one-place-you-can't-brush-your-teeth-until-the-second-show. The strangers pulling at you because they love you but you having no love to give back. The singing the same songs night after night, day after day, and if you read the gossip columns the rumors that your husband is only after your fame. The wondering if your children will be glad to see you and maybe the not caring if they are. The scheming to get out of just one show and go just one place where some dodo dupadeduke won't say, "Just sing one song, please." Nobody mentions how it feels to become a freak because you have talent, and how no one gives a damn how you feel but only cares that maybe Aretha Franklin is here, like it's the new cure for cancer. And if you say you're lonely or scared or tired how they probably always say just "Oh, come off it" or "Did you see how they love you—did you see?" Which most likely has nothing to do with you anyway.

And I'm not saying Aretha shouldn't have talent and I'm certainly not saying she should quit singing, but as much as I love to see her I'd vote yes (if someone asked) to have her do three or four concerts a year, stay home or do whatever she wants and make records, because I think it's a shame the way we are killing her. We eat up artists like there's going to be a famine in three minutes when there are in fact an abundance of talents just waiting. Let's put some of the giants away for a while and deal with them as though they have a life to lead. Aretha doesn't have to relive Billie Holiday's life or Dinah Washington's death. But who is there to stop the pattern? She's more important than her music if they must be separated, and they should be separated when she has to pass out before anyone will recognize she needs a rest. And I say this because I need Aretha's music. She is undoubtedly the one person who put everybody on notice. Aretha sings "I Say a Little Prayer" and Dionne doesn't even want to hear it anymore. Aretha sings "Money Won't Change You" but James Brown won't sing "Respect." The advent of Aretha pushed brother Ray Charles back to singing the blues. Made Dionne quit fooling and stick to movie themes. Made Diana Ross get an Afro wig. Pushed Black singers who were negro into their negroness and all others into Blackness. You couldn't jive when Aretha said, "Woman's only human." The Blazers said, "Gotta let a man be a man." When Aretha took the stage the blues were "rediscovered." There has been no musician her very presence hasn't affected. When she told Humphrey to go fly a kite he pressured James Brown. They removed Otis because the combination was too strong. The Impressions said, "We're a Winner." The Black songs started coming from not only the singers on stage but the dancers in the streets. Aretha was a riot. Was the leader. If she had said, come, let's do it, it would have been done. And this was not unnoted by insignificant others. It should also be noted by us.

Two years ago John A. Williams published a novel called *The Man Who Cried I Am*, which contained two significant parts and one significant line. The line is "How should we do it [kill Max]? They can't all die of overdoses." And this means a lot to us when we realize the number of musicians we've lost in Europe to overdoses. But it also has meaning for us when we realize that John Coltrane died. Musicians have always been in the forefront of the Black experience. Long before the advent of the X seekers musicians were naming themselves with African names (Ahmad Jamal, Yusef Lateef). Music has been the voice of the Black experience most especially here in America. And an important voice was stilled. Many important voices one way or the other have been stilled.

Coltrane was easily understood if you understand Black people. Insignificant others recorded him and slowed the tapes to a crawl —they still couldn't chart how many notes he would hit with one breath. And I say John Coltrane played the blues because the blues are what we sing to ourselves. You can't hum *Ascension* all alone but a group of you can create your own salvation. That's all he's saying. And it comes through loud and clear. And if it's disturbing that's because the truth generally is. Coltrane isn't another kind of soul—he is soul. How can you separate food from thought? Sex from salvation? The mind from the body? They are all one. And John Coltrane brought them together. Garland continuously delineates, tries to say this is one kind of soul and that another or that isn't true soul. It's a whole bunch of foolishness because our music is Black music. Call it work song, Gospel, spiritual, jazz, R&B, Liberation music. It is Black music created by Black people to let other Black people know what we feel, what we are thinking. All the rest is about how white people react to our expression.

The last chapter, "The Sound of Soul To Come," is particularly weak because Garland ignores Liberation Music and opts for universal (whatever that means) music. She ignores Sun Ra's Space Music, which children really love. And sort of overlooks the crying need for the groups to come back. The youngsters are still harmonizing on the corners and our music will still be determined by our condition.

I'm sure *The Sound of Soul* will be read, as all books by Black people should be read. We've spoken recently a lot about the need for us to criticize ourselves, and this can only be done if we know what we are criticizing. We find Garland to be a little off base and hope that the book on R&B will still be done. Just as Cruse has accused the intellectuals of the 1930s of holding back Black people, we feel that Garland is saying, if we just had a few more white people singing the blues all would be right with the world. I'm sure if that were the case no singer would be without an insignificant other in his group; but that is not the case. The music was born because of our treatment by others, and the more they steal it the more they prove how little regard they have for us. The more we support their thievery the more we show what little regard we have for ourselves. Sly says, "Thank you for the party but I could never stay." That's a soul sound.

12

Convalescence—Compared to What? *

In the beginning was the rape
And the rape was labored
And the embryo was cleaved
From the womb
And the painful journey
Across the ice
Began

PERHAPS THE BIGGEST QUESTION in the modern world is the definition of a genus—huemanity. And the white man is no hueman. It's sheer stupidity for America to be in Vietnam—win, lose (which we are all doing) or draw—because only David can win when Goliath accepts the challenge. It's like men playing women in basketball; after all, they are men. But it's questionable whether the honkie has a mind. He is an illogical animal. Animals in their natural environment have friends and enemies; live in a circumscribed place; travel by one or two methods—if they swim and fly they don't run; create little animal communities; live and die. The honkie has defied all this and forced us to defy it. Honkies can eat anything with impunity—witness pigs, snakes, snails, each other, their children. They have made one form of cannibalism a love act, which just has to be a comment on their ability to understand word meanings. It's difficult

*Reprinted from Mel Watkins, ed., *Black Review No. 1*, New York, William Morrow & Company, Inc., 1971, pp. 117–128.

to define a honkie. We all remember zombie movies, the big, black, dead things under the bidding of the evil scientist moving around in the jungles of Haiti or some island (it is always an island) hating themselves for what they are but powerless to put their bodies down to rest. Generally an ugly honkie woman, which of course is redundant, comes along who is taken to the zombie hideout and Wild Bill Hickok in safari hat and bush jacket follows her, finds the secret of how to kill the zombie (how can you kill something already dead?) and runs back to civilization. Now, the zombie is a drink. You order it when you really want to tie one on. Wouldn't it be marvelous if we could run to the neighborhood bar and say, "Give me a double honkie on the rocks, Sam," and have the bartender pour something into a mixer and shake it up? Something needs to shake up the honkie. And a lot of negroes too.

When someone looks at the Watusi and thinks that's the totality of our contribution to the world we realize we are in trouble. Not that we are against the Watusi—personally we favor ass shaking under even the most mundane circumstances—but the Watusi is a religious dance performed ritualistically by the high priest and priestess of soul. And just as the Roeman Catholic Church will not allow the unanointed to partake of the blood and body we should set up the same standards. A people cannot accept as a sign of health nonbelievers practicing their service. This is the crisis Harold Cruse speaks of and a gross abdication of our duties. Those of us who have studied and feel compelled to speak on issues should speak the whole, not the hole, truth.

O ye of little faith and less knowledge, let us venture forth into the night, you with your Fanon and I with my twat in the hand.

In the beginning was the man and the man was Black and the Black man was a good man. In the beginning was the woman and the woman was Black and the Black woman was a good woman. They had children, planted, reaped, lived, died. Maybe drank a little bali hai, were late on the rent, probably had some kind of car, educated the children—were men and women. Black and proud,

"Say it loud." They meditated on the sun and planets, created a number system; meditated on the earth and figured if they could get a lever they could tilt it. Figured out how deep was the ocean, how to mummify people, that Anacin was the best thing for a headache ("Butter? Butter? Bitch, you know we ain't had no butter since yo' daddy left us!"); charted the seasons, figured out astrology—the Sphinx is Virgo and Leo no matter what honkies say about their not going together; lived in peace, blended with the earth, had children . . . lived . . . died . . . continued. Then, Buffy tells us, a buzzard came along, sucked the eggs and changed the story.

Man can't separate the mind from the body, sex from salvation, food from thought—the supermasculine menial does not exist. There is no such thing as the omnipotent administrator—what is a superbrain? The pope is the queen of the earth. We are a complete people ready and able to deal completely with tomorrow. We are lovers and children of lovers. We are warriors and children of warriors. But we don't send children to war. No crusades to hold back the Muslim tides. No crusades to hold back the union forces. The child's place is in the home though we, as children, seized the initiative here in America. The Black family in America has never been declining. When the honkie speaks of the deteriorating negro family he's wrong on all counts. We are not negro. We are not deteriorating; our structure has always been the extended family—many generations living under one roof. Our structure has generally been matrilineal, though seldom matriarchal. What does the Black woman have to be powerful with/over? If ever you see a powerful nonwhite know that you are seeing a powerful negro. Then ask yourself . . . what's a negro?

The honkie is the best mythologist in creation. He's had practice because his whole wrap is to protect himself from his environment. After generations of lying he does it by second nature. And his first nature is so unnatural that we aren't surprised. "Fish gotta swim, birds gotta fly"—honkies gotta lie. I'm telling you why.

Black people are calypso singers; call us signifiers. Carolyn

Rodgers and Larry Neal say Shine swam on. Rap Brown played ball in Central Park and Shine swims on. The ultrafeminine and the supermasculine menial—no good. I can't use it. "Try to make it real compared to what?" It ain't real—we can't even pronounce the words they and some of us are using to describe us. "What you mean, castrated? Oh, yeah. Well, I been that." Bullshit. Try to make it real. "My mother did what? Man, you better watch yo' mouth." Goddammit! Compared to what? (Un)Les McCann can't. Honk on, Pharaoh—that's for real. Compared to anything. Sock it toward me now.

Oh, we're so angry with you, America; ask Buck White. "I gotta live the life I sing about in my songs." Marion Williams and the sweet Inspirations. Electric Mud and the Dells saying, "Oh, What a Night." They were in Washington, D. C., April 5, 1968. Souls on ice, but "To be black," Don Lee says, "is to be very hot." The age of the cool went out when honkies learned to say "dig" with their eyelids lowered. All we got left is motherfucker. F(or) u(se) (of) c (arnal) k(nowledge). They can never get that together.

A slave is defined by his duties. And none of us is free. The guns should be toward the West. Nix(on) him. Spear o Agnew. Won't we ever learn? Elijah says we are what we eat. The time is overdue to close the doors. It's overdue time to say which nigger is our nigger. That's all that matters. Support our own. Look out for our own. Yeah, turn the system Black. Don't be afraid of Black folks. Don't be afraid of yo' mama. She ain't the one who put you in this trick. But she's the one who'll get you out. And we aren't speaking genetically. We are all fathers and mothers. Mother is the earth, father the tool to fertilize her. We/they go hand in hand.

In the beginning of the honkie the word was God and the word was white. The paper was white so the word couldn't be seen but only felt. Take away the damned and you get evil. DEVIL. Take away the damned. Some were taught the devil is Black. We're taught he's red. By any definition of devil *she's* got to be white. Only the devil could cause so much heartache.

Roaches are red,
The sky is now blue.
If you ain't gone by night
We're gonna lynch you.

The original white poem. And some Black folks think whites can write.

It's a cinch we didn't need to read their shit. Why would Dostoevski need to write *Crime and Punishment?* For the same reason Shakespeare needed to write—not to pass information but to pass time. There are no great honkies—anything that excludes our existence is not great. Anything that sheds a negative light on us isn't great. Faulkner was a racist. Not even a great racist—just a Southerner who had no useful skills. Didn't even write well. The best you can say for an imitator is that he copies well. For true knowledge we must go to the source. Camus and Sartre dig on existentialism because it relieves them of guilt and allows them to colonize Fanon and other Blacks under the name of philosophy. Without existentialism they would just be honkie colonizers. Existentialism became popular after World War II when it was obvious that the world had changed colors. German collaborators, honkies who refused to speak out for the Jews (though speaking out wasn't nearly ever going to be enough), Jews who refused to speak out for the Jews all turned to a philosophy that would allow them to be responsible for the world in general and nothing in particular.

Black groups digging on white philosophies ought to consider the source. Know who's playing the music before you dance. Someone's poem said, before you go to the water know who invented the beach. Brothers digging on class struggle ought to go check out African communalism. That warmed-over communism which allowed Russia to become a modern, industrialized, capitalistic state isn't for or about us. It's just an old way of colonizing us. "Pussycat, pussycat, I love you," and some of us are falling for that. Some of us seem ready to accept the essence without performing the act.

Can't be done. If they had such great minds how come their country is falling apart? James Earl Jones notwithstanding—America is the great white hope. And she's building a country home in South Africa where the weather is cooler. And people talk about not accepting dirty money. All money is dirty. Dirty, lazy, filthy lucre. Money don't work. Money don't sing. Money don't dance. Can't keep you warm. Money is a leech. And we drain ourselves to obtain her. Have fallen in love with her. Will put no other god before her. Try to make it real. Compare the gold in Fort Knox in bars to the way our bodies used to shine with ornaments. Yeah, we are the body and the blood. We are the salvation. But we too need a transplant. Vital organs cannot survive in a decaying body.

Melvin Tolson says a civilization is in decline when we (they) begin to judge it. The Visigoths didn't destroy Rome; they just got there in time to claim historical credit. Who will get credit for America? That's what the struggle is all about. Some say niggers twisting will cause the decline; some say that will save it. But this old body is dying all on its own and we must decide whether we are going to take credit for giving it its last kick or for being the last group to try to save it. If I saw a sick old white lady on her way to a convalescence home I'd kick her in the ass and rob her of the twenty cents her dollar is worth—and be proud that I'd done it. No sense trying to save sick old white ladies. Try to make it real. Young white people will even kick an old, sick white lady on her way to the convalescence home because they want to take credit for being the cause of the fall. Compared to what?

There was peace after the fall of Rome. Roads fell into disuse. Weeds covered them. The aqueducts dried up. The soldiers turned their swords into plows. There was no central authority. There was no standard. Southern Italians were glad Rome was dead. They went back to drinking wine, having babies, educating children. Living. Dying. They spoke Italian. Roman mercenaries in France stopped collecting taxes. Learned French. Started drinking wine. People crossed the Channel. People moved into the Black Forest.

The Visigoths moved on. And all was quiet on the Western front. Then some bright dude decided to write a book in vernacular. And in Italy the Renaissance was born. What had been a period of peace was deemed the Dark Ages. What had been a democratic period was called anarchy. The rich got poor and the poor got happy. And happy got his ass kicked for coming to the neighborhood. You see it now. The Black Renaissance is born. Joy to the world.

LeRoi Jones moved uptown. Wrote plays in the vernacular and a people found our voice. The idea and the essence had finally formed the man. But the separation was never mind from body. It was body from function. The mind always knew what needed to be done. It wasn't a stupid nigger that fucked with Nat Turner. It wasn't a stupid nigger that killed Malcolm. It's too easy to say how dumb we are. All we got is rhythm. Giving the twist to the world will not change that world. And it's far from what we have given. Our bodies—in fields, in offices, in laboratories, in beds, in Harlem, Watts, Accra, LondonParisRomeCincinnati—laid to sacrifice will not change the world.

Young whites deciding to get hold of our rhythm and fuck will not change the world. It's a physical change and chemical warfare is needed. We need to put a hurting on the world. And all our intellecting about changes are gonna come, "Yeah, baby, let me . . . let me, baby," will not change the world. Swapping sweat or spit, even wallowing in the shit together, may at best allow some honkies to try to sing the blues—which we would all do all the time if we knew what we don't want to know. The blues, Mae Jackson tells me, ain't what they used to be—done gone and got Americanized. And we know that's a shame. Come telling Mae to stay in school. Ain't that a bitch? Her what never went to no institution at all, telling her to stay in school, and the most tragic thing that happens in America is that there is an accident on the Pneu Jersey Turnpike.

Ever think about waking up facing Lieutenant William L. Calley? Well, we'd better be thinking about it because they brought that cracker home as punishment for being so stupid. They're gonna force that cracker to listen to the Temps saying, "I Can't Get Next to You." And Calley'll be nodding, "You said it, nigger." It's all there in the big black book called *Whatever Happened to Cracker America?* Ruth ain't no Baby and her daddy would rather you not eat it —some things are just bad form. Squash it together and you get bath. Squash it at all and you'll need one. The biggest lie in creation is, you shouldn't try to keep up with the Joneses. LeRoi, Sandy, their mama and daddy are something to aspire to. The cracker will take everything away from you if you don't be careful. Woodie King is pure mahogany. The single most important theatrical event aside from Watts, Newark and Detroit was his production of *Slave Ship*.

It's so easy to deal off the top. Sly says dance to the music. A compelling call to do the freedom walk. But we're still dealing on the catch-up. Crackers have taken our blues and gone. Langston saw it a long time ago. Taken our blues and put long hair on it. Electrified it. They're gonna go in for electric dicks next. Gonna put them at thirty-three rpms. All they gotta remember to do is turn the heart up to "Excitement," turn the brain to "Profanity." Ain't gonna be much running off natural rhythm. Just like Anton Dvořák took our spirituals and put them in symphony, they're putting our blues in symphony hall. Yes, they is—saw the sign up in Newark. You see it now—the Grateful Dead—living proof. Of the Grateful Dead. Give a cracker a break—in the neck. And pan-broil it with Black eyes of sympathetic niggers; should make a good meal for the conjure man. Try to make it real.

Niggers got a natural twist, especially when we hanging from a wild oak tree. Ever hear a real Black person extol the virtues of nature? If you do you'll know it's a negro talking. Nature ain't natural here. Growing big Black niggers from trees. Running down country roads. Trying to make it to the swamp. Niggers love cement. And there's a reason. If little old men with eight heads came from Mars New Yorkers would send Lindsay down to see what they want. Absolute faith in the new politics. Rah-rah, Lindsay. Anyone Nixon hates has got to be good. Apollo got nothing to do with space; ask any Black kid from 110th Street to 155th. The Apollo now features Dionne Warwicke with her love show.

Determined weakness will triumph over the most brilliant, strong-willed purist. There's something about weakness that always seems to make it prevail. Call it arrogance. Most strong people think they can reason with the weak—call it *noblesse oblige*. Most strong people think the least they can do is bend a little—call it illogic. Most strong people have no real knowledge of how their strength is used against them. The cracker is a weak being. So is the negro. Both sap the energies of Black people. The best anyone can do when dealing with weakness is to get as far away from it as possible. Learn to steel yourself against terms like *evil* (the weak always tell the strong it's evil to be strong). Learn to say, "That's true," when the weak say, "You don't love me." But mostly learn to deal with other strong people.

Jesus on the cross knew the weak have a league, a Thursday Night Weak Club, where they devise new and exciting ways to trap the strong. And we accept it. The weak have made *selfish* the worst possible name to be called. Couple *selfish* with *nigger* and there is no lower animal under Allah's wig. The weak have made cleanliness next to godliness and God a green faggot who fucked nature and set the world in motion. The weak have made weakness a religion. The weaker you are the more you have a right to drain the strong. The weak worship weakness. They thrive on it. They love it. Next to death weakness is all they respect. You are what you love. The weak have weakness built into the system. There's no way to beat the system. There's no way to change the system. Only you change. Only you begin to think it's not so bad. Only you become weaker because the weak have made strength mean ineffectualness, have made it mean exile, have made it mean jail, have made it mean loneliness, misunderstanding, negativeness. The only good strong person is a dead strong person and weakness kills us dead. God is dead. Jesus is dead. Allah is dead. King is dead. Malcolm is dead. Coltrane is dead. Dolphy is dead. Evers is dead. And we write poems to them. Sing songs to them. Pour gin libations to them. Miss them. Quote them. While we don't give a kind word to Mingus, the Aylers, Aretha, Ameer Baraka, Adam Powell.

Like we don't know what mess James Brown is going through. Like we don't know how A. D. King died. Like we don't like each other because we look alike. And like the book says, "Nothing black but a Cadillac." Niggers ought to be buried in Cadillacs because that's what's killing us. GM, Brooks Brothers, Lord & Taylor, VWs, Carrier air-conditioning, Philco "new color" TV with the works in a box—does your box work when you want it to? Get a Philco for your box. We've got to quit worshipping weakness. We've got to quit understanding it. We've got to quit accepting it. We've got to be strong. In a world where the weak function the strong must not function. We need togetherness to decide what we will do when they are gone. And we must help them go.

We need to devise a way to put Black teenage girls to work on the trains. Old Black people traveling on the East Coast take their lives in their hands. Are unable to make changes of trains. In the South and West buses are full of our elderly people. Why can't young ladies ride the trains/buses for the express purpose of helping these people? Why don't bus companies provide space for them and the state pay them to travel with our elderly citizens? It would help make the elders more comfortable. Why don't we have our young men with some kind of machine cleaning the subways? That could be a twenty-four-hour thing. The subs are filthy and unsafe. Why not put our youngsters to work for a four-hour shift with the state paying them to do it? New Yorkers will suffocate before the bomb drops. Why don't we close the streets, plant grass and leave only the avenues for traffic? We need to outlaw cars in the cities. Transportation could then be by bus with alternate avenues running up and down. You would never be more than a block from where you're going. Traffic jams would be no more. The air would be cleaner. Our children would have someplace to play. We need in all the big cities to have daily garbage and trash collection. We need to make the buildings we live in safe and habitable. We need to put our women to work sewing curtains, making quilts, cooking, keeping house. Our men need to repair, renovate, renew the neighborhood. We need to abolish by declaration private everything: housing, property, companies, clubs, you name it—it should go. Everything should be in trust for the people. And what the people don't keep up we don't need. We need to spend as much money feeding people as we do starving them. We need to spend as much time devising ways for people to live as we do for killing people.

Crackers invented Napalm, which is so hot it can melt your skin, but they can't deal with a decent ice defroster when it snows. We need a shift in priorities. And only we can bring it if it can be brought. And not by taking on their weakness but by building our own nation. And if a nation can't be built here, by preparing to live without the nonessentials, which we've never had and are better off without. We may in fact miss the refrigerator, but compare that to air pollution. It all goes together. The refrigerator you need today is keeping Nixon in office. Will put Agnew in office. This is the fall of America. The Kennedys were the Gracchus brothers; America is Rome. The end is the beginning. We must think small, organize small, do little things to chip away at this monolith, and Elvis Presley ain't gonna make it easier. We must recognize that most countries could fit into any American state. America is an unnatural city state run by unnatural people. We must huddle together in our similarities, develop our language, develop our life style, quit trying to impress the cracker and try to be happy. We must bring on the Dark Ages when Dark people rule. When, better still, there is no rule—only Black people living, giving birth, rearing children, dying, continuing the life pattern in a natural way. We need new definitions and the twist ain't got nothing to do with it. It's time to work to pull down the walls—yeah, it's time for Atlas to shrug so that Atlas Junior can live.

13

Gemini—a Prolonged Autobiographical Statement on Why

IN THE BEGINNING, I'm told, earth was one with the sun. One bright hot ball in the middle of space whirling, whirling, whizzing around God like a smooth Bob Gibson strike. Then for reasons yet unexplained—maybe earth got bored with hot space balls—it pulled away and flew, as Mercury and Mars had done, from the mother sun. Since it was so young and inexperienced it didn't want to leave by itself so it coaxed Venus to come also. It settled in an all-white neighborhood between its brother and sister. Now, there isn't much a terribly hot planet can do all alone in space (being Christian and knowing incest is unacceptable) so earth cooled down. After a few thousand years it wanted something to play with so it invented man. I'm told on good authority by the Holy Ghost Company, Inc., one of our oldest census bureaus, that man was formed of many materials in different places at the same time. There were, however, three basic molds. The soil out of which the African was molded worked out to be the best. The standard was set by him. That's why mankind is called hueman beings.

The Oriental had a majestic manner and felt little or no need to involve himself with the rest of the earth. He set up trading with Africa and created an elitist mentality which wasn't necessarily imperialistic so God gave him gunpowder and explosives to play with. The European was always cold. All the time. He developed a gutsy quality which would help him survive almost no matter what. He learned to eat anything, go anyplace, and being basically mischievous how to destroy everything he didn't understand. God got a little bored with the antics of the Europeans and in the very first mass punishment of man sent the Ice Age to Europe.

The curse of the Nordics trailed them all the way to the northern tip of Africa. The first thing the Europeans wanted to know was, how come the Africans didn't have no ice age? And a very wise African guru who just happened to be visiting in the city at that time said, "Son, look at the Sahara Desert. We had a city there called York which was great and held many different peoples. It was a pleasant city run by a friendly mayor who could not quite get along with either the president of the republic or the governor of the province. The friendly mayor wanted more parks, more space, but trading was plentiful so more and more businesses went up and more asphalt was laid and more people from the surrounding countryside had to come in to work. Eventually they choked the land to death and the desert came in. This was a great tragedy and I am here to tell the Europeans of our loss."

The Nordics were so impressed and excited they decided to go to Africa to study and learn so that they would not make the same mistake. "May we go back with you to study and learn? Then we can tell our people." "But there are only two of you," the African replied, "and one is female." "Yeah, that's the only way we could escape the ice. They let one male and one female of each species on the great sled." "But how will you tell your people of what happened?" "Oh, don't worry," said the Nordic. "We have a thing called writing." "Writing? I have never heard of this." "Oh, it's a thing we learned when we lived in caves. We're a nocturnal people, you know, so during the daytime we began drawing on walls. Then we moved on to creating an alphabet. Now we write novels, poems and plays, not to mention short stories and legal documents, and we've invented a thing we call money. Fantastic! The best possible system for man to live under."

"Well, young man . . . and young lady . . . despite our being an oral people we have a method we developed during your Ice Age called hieroglyphics. It consists of—"

"Nothing like our writing. With our writing we tell our truth."

"But young man, you didn't let me tell about our hieroglyphics. Now, as I was saying—"

"Old man, it's nothing like what we have. We tell our truth. We are setting world standards of beauty, politics, love, literature. . . . We will control everything with our writing."

"Young man, you are rude and boorish. This 'writing' of yours will get you nowhere. If you would mind your manners and respect your elders you would go farther."

"You wait and see, Sage, we're going to change the world. You may think you have something like it but you don't. We're telling our truth. You tell yours. Our writing will get us over. Just you wait and see." And unfortunately it did. And for a long time. Which is primarily why I became poetically inclined.

People always write you and ask how you got to be or how you became a writer or a poet. And sometimes I'm in a really good mood and I say, "Because I have no other skills," and they always, I mean always, laugh and say, "Yes, but how?" And that's the truth—I can't do anything else that well. If I could have held a job down in Walgreen's I probably would have and would have fantasied myself into believing that selling that perfume somehow made the world a more perfect place. I was always that kind of salesman. It's like starting out in your life with the idea that whatever you do is so crucial to the world. . . .

Emperors, heads of state, beautiful, chic ladies all came to Walgreen's on Linn Street to have me sell them the correct perfume. Then when they moved me to the front cash register I was a princess from a foreign country, not Europe or Asia but somewhere deep in the Afro-Carib or something, and my parents had sent me to learn about this America. It was at times a bit dull, at times very hard work but the test was, could I get through it? Could I, a being from almost another planet, communicate that it is all in good hands, I am here checking you out of this store? And I would laugh and talk, giving, as I thought a princess should, a little sun on an otherwise dreary day. And sometimes when I was tired or a bit lonely or afraid I would be tempted to turn to my bagger and say, "This isn't really me. . . . I'm a princess and my parents are testing me by having me in this city in this store and one day you will all know who I really am." But that's like getting the big end of the wishbone and then telling the wish. The real task was not the work but my identity. Could I maintain my silence? Could I alone keep myself intact? And I tried to perform to the utmost.

I did have a friend and people would say, what you are doing for Claudia is wonderful, and I wanted to say, but she's doing me a favor, because I didn't have many friends and have always been truly grateful for those few I have. And she went on to finish high school and my mother would say, you have really helped Claudia, and I would say, without her I would have gone insane. Which is more or less true because people or at least I cannot live without someone. That's one reason my son means so much to me. I finally have someone who knows me and isn't awed or afraid and I can love him completely and not feel that I'll be abused or misunderstood. Most people go through life never daring to say just one time, "Fuck it, I'm going to love you." And I can really understand why because the minute you do you open yourself. And sometimes you say, that's all right; if he takes advantage of me, so what? At nineteen that's cool. Or maybe at twenty-three. But around twenty-five or thirty you say, maybe men and women aren't meant to live with each other. Maybe they have a different sort of thing going where they come together during mating season and produce beautiful, useless animals who then go on to love, you hope, each of you . . . but living together there are too many games to be gotten through. And the intimacies still seem to be left to his best friend and yours. I mean, the incidence is too high to be ignored. The guy and girl are inseparable until they get married; then he's out with his friends and she's out with hers or home alone, and there is no reason to think he's lying when he says he loves her. . . . She's just not the other half of him. He is awed and frightened by her screams and she is awed and cautious about his tears. Which is not to say there is not one man or one woman who can't make a marriage—i.e., home—run correctly and maybe even happily but it happens so infrequently. Or as a relative of mine in one of her profound moments said, "Marriage is give and take—you give and he takes." And I laughed because it was the kind of hip thing I was laughing about then. And even if that's true, so what? Somebody has to give and somebody has to take. But people set roles out, though the better you play them the more useless you are to that person. People move in conflicts. To me sex is an essence. . . . It's a basic of hueman relationships. And sex is conflict; it could be considered a miniwar between two people. Really. I think so. So I began to consider being a writer.

I used to spend time in Indianapolis when I was younger. It was referred to by us as Naptown. And saying I had spent the weekend in Nap always made me feel I had done something. Then too my aunt, unlike my mother, was socially aggressive so we always knew the really in people . . . and even if I didn't no one knew that I didn't. So I could continue my fantasy about who I was and what my purpose was without going through the hard fact that somebody would know. What I regret most about modern children is that their imagination is stifled so early. City living is barely fit for adults and surely must be considered unfit for children. Where do the dreams be born? Where do you go for privacy? If a city child walks the streets alone what mother in her right mind wouldn't be worried? Not that the crackers in the suburbs or on farms are any different. Theirs is the ugliness that makes our cities unsafe and I would imagine it affects them.

When I was little we had an outdoor toilet which I only vaguely remember, but I do know sitting on the john was hip. I clearly remember that. Sitting and daydreaming about all the important heads of states and movie stars waiting for me, an essentially poor sort of muddy-colored colored girl, to emerge. I could hold the whole world up if I so chose. But with power comes responsibility and my grandmother, who was one of the world's greatest women, taught me my responsibility to my people. I would emerge to give Cab Calloway his turn or mostly Nellie Lutcher or Billy Eckstine, since they were the big favorites. Sometimes after we moved to a better apartment it would be Jimmy Edwards. I vividly remember *Home of the Brave*. Mommy got my sister and me all dressed up to go to town. I got sick on the bus to my mortification and everyone else's discomfort and had to be recleaned. I had a blue teddy-bear coat, a white muff and three plaits—and I was going with my mama and my sister to the white show downtown. We made it. Mostly the movie is foggy but Jimmy Edwards was a soldier coming home from war and he was beaten up. Mommy told Gary or maybe no one at all, "It's a damn shame." And Gary was crying. I remember Jimmy Edwards staggering probably home and I was in a rage. Then we left and had dinner at Mr. Patton's barbecue place on Ninth Street and came home. It was a fabulous muff and I loved the coat. But the rage stayed with me.

And when I was a little girl with mostly big eyes and high-top shoes people would come up to me and say, "Nikki, can you read?" And I'd proudly answer, "No. But Gary can." And they'd say, "Nikki, can you sing?" And I'd let my chest swell a bit and say, "No. But Gary can." Then they, I would imagine laughing at me though I didn't know it then, would say, "Nikki, can you play the piano?" And I would lean back on my heels and smile as if I had this one clinched too and say, "No. But Gary can!" And it really knocked me out that I knew someone who could do all those marvelous things they asked about. And sometimes someone would think to ask, "Well, what do you do?" And I'd say, "I'm Gary's sister!" If I hadn't been taught to be respectful to older people I would have added, "Dummy." I was Gary's sister and that really was quite enough. And I don't think I could have survived without that as a buffer. I watched the world through her eyes and saw what she saw and what I saw. And the family would say, "You're a fool about Gary. She's gonna use you." And I never understood that to be bad. I mean, if you must be used it should be by someone you love. So I would always say, "Just to keep the record straight, if I had eight pints of blood and Gary needed ten I'd take two from you and give her my eight." It seemed perfectly logical to feel that way about your sister. Mommy always told us we only had each other. Maybe that's why Gary's been married five times and I none.

I don't think I idolize her as much anymore. As a matter of fact our relationship hit a mature high when in the fifth grade she beat me up for wearing her clothes. I decided then and there we would shift to a sounder base. I would cease wearing her clothes and she would cease beating me up. I was badder than she anyway so clearly I let her win. That level of dishonesty can destroy any feeling so we drew a line in the room defining her half and my half with the vow never to cross it and settled down to be friends. I still dig Gary more than anyone outside Tommy. And recognizing that love requires careful nourishing we keep a safe distance, coming together to share happiness and sadness but never making judgments or giving advice to each other. "You ain't got no sense when it comes to her," even my grandmother used to say, but of course I did—I decided to feel about her and her life as she wanted me to and to do what she wanted me to do, and she gave this to me. What else are your people for?

We had to deal with Mommy's reaction to her own value system. Gary and I had a tendency to close her out. I think fathers are generally a little jealous of their children and mothers skirt a twilight zone between loyalties. But mothers give a lot to their little ones and are quite naturally closer to them than fathers. Mothers say, "If you don't buy the kids new skates for Christmas I'm going to find someone who will," and things like that to threaten fathers and then mothers turn around and find out that the very people they have gone down behind are closing them out. It must be a tremendous blow. That's why I don't believe in altruism. Nobody in his right mind would do anything unless it was better for him because the minute you try to go against your feelings to help someone you get shitted on. So I would slyly hint from behind one of those history books I used to be hung up with that it's best to do what is best for you and then you never have to expect something back because the something was inherent in your action. And Mommy would look at me and say, "I have given my life for you children," and I used to take it to heart and pledge my life to her until I understood that what she really meant wasn't what she was saying and what she really wanted us to do was to produce great, beautiful grandchildren and leave her the hell alone with our father. That's why it's dangerous for Black people to take English too seriously.

My fantasy life went on with a different personality emerging all the time. But I was always grand in my cowboy boots or grinding in Johnetta's rathskeller at parties. I was always just a little secreted away with the thought that one day I would be understood. This is probably a main reason any artist emerges.

I've been slow to make evaluations. My life style was that I read about fifty books a year and absorbed them and then related them to another level. And I tried to read Black books. I remember reading "Annie Allen" and being pleased for the first time with poetry. But I didn't pursue it. I went on to Pound and Eliot because it filled an empty spot in my head while not upsetting my emotions. I felt at some point I would probably have a nervous breakdown; then I recognized how aesthetically unattractive that was so I divorced reason from feeling and moved on. Mommy asked me to read three books, one of which was *Black Boy*. I took it to school in the seventh grade and the nun called it trash. Which was beautiful. Because I could intellectually isolate all white nuns as being dumb and unworthy of my attention. I fell madly in love with a Black one, however, which probably just testifies to my hopeless hopeful- ness that there is some validity in everything. And I was really turned on to Greek and Roman mythology—the gods and god- desses towering over everybody in their exclusive god club. And I would think if ever I was a goddess I would take it all seriously, and not eat pomegranates or fall in love with anyone other than a god and I would bear proud sons and train them correctly. I would learn from mistakes and if not eradicate them completely then at least create new ones. It seemed only reasonable.

And one thing I recognized quite some time ago is that no one makes a mistake. Yeah, you can show someone 1^1 plus 1^1 equals 2^2 or something like that but even scientists are reluctant to assert the earth was never flat or the molecule was never the smallest par- ticle of matter. And I think we are in error when we begin with the assumption that we can show someone—anyone—the error of his ways. It's like with parents. No matter what a fuck-up goof-off you turn out to be they only have two reactions available to them: (1) there is nothing wrong with you or (2) they did their best. Mothers of murderers, rapists, thieves, psychopaths, corporate executives, presidents all say the same things. Tell your parents you're sick. They will finally, if you really beat them down, make one of those two statements.

Same with white folks. We started out thinking if we showed them how hurt, sick, misused or abused we were they would change their ways. Their response has been (1) there is nothing wrong with colored folks or (2) they did the best they could. It's only natural. And what we have to decide is whether we want to make them face the truth as we see it or to control our lives for our own goals. Those are two different objectives. One is for losing; one is for winning. Because it really doesn't matter, if you want to control, whether they understand or not—parents or white folks. It only matters that their behavior changes. And the way some of us conduct our lives we'd be at a loss if anything happened to our antagonists, you know? If all the white folks disappeared tomorrow a whole lot of us would be lost—but it shouldn't matter.

Same with kids who act out their parents' sickness. So you're twenty-five years old and were too severely toilet-trained. It's already happened. And you can run it down from every angle but it's your life and even if your mother says she's sorry you have to live with reality. Or worse, if they die you have no antagonist. You/we all must learn to live for ourselves.

In a rational system this means living for our people. But with the realization that we are our people. I'm always amazed at the Julia–Diana Ross discussion as if we would somehow become "free" if they somehow became "Black." So we spend a lot of time knocking people who perhaps don't go along with us as opposed to helping people who do. It's like the plain Jane who just has to have the football hero—not that she can't get who she wants, you understand, but why climb over five guys who want you for one who doesn't? Or negroes who need crackers to say, "Well done." Same syndrome. Why not try to deal with the folks who want to deal with you? It's self-hatred always to be chasing after what never was.

I never wanted to be Ralph Ellison. The piece James Mac-Pherson did on him in the *Atlantic* was pitiful. He's not worth it—and when we have to give up an issue of a vital magazine to explain the one book he wrote it shows where we're coming from. Especially when there has been no issue on John Killens (four books) or John Williams (eight books) or James Baldwin (nine books) or any of the people who are continuing to write and take chances. The only single book worth that much space is the Bible and it's an anthology. In so many subtle ways we do ourselves an injustice. If Ellison's book was that great he should have won a Pulitzer Prize (Harper Lee did). If he wrote all that well he should keep writing. But he didn't. Which is the main basis on which I judge his work. As a novel *Invisible Man* is good; as a writer Ellison is so much hot air, because he hasn't had the guts to go on writing. But he can put us down and say we are not writers. Us—the Rodgerses, Marshalls, Reeds and others who are persistently exposing our insides and trying to create a reality. And I don't think all the writing out there is so dynamite. But I respect to the utmost the chances taken. Any one of us could pick our best work, present it and lay back. But we didn't/have not. We've gone on to write bad poems as well as other good ones, to write copout novels as well as stirring pieces—we've gone on to create a literature, to be hueman in our failures as well as glorious in our successes. But mostly we've continued. And I think that's what counts.

For whatever reason—one I hope to understand before I evolve into a turtle (my next form)—Black folks always seem to think there is one answer for one problem. Not only is that ludicrous to me but generally the right question hasn't been asked in the first place. Mankind is a morass of mistakes. His intellect has always outstripped his emotional growth. For some reason people still seem to find it easier to hate than to love, easier to kill than to help live, easier to control and abort than to allow and nourish.

And I believe the white man is a natural man, that his anxieties and fears are the anxieties and fears of natural men, because I watch us going into the same syndromes. I'm forced now to admit the white woman is obviously a natural and perhaps superior piece cause I have watched and am watching our men go ape shit to get it. Panthers coalescing and Communists communing are still talking about getting a white piece. And if it costs them their lives as it has been costing our men their cultural, emotional, spiritual and physical lives, that appears to be a small enough price to pay for it. Black men are having a prolonged love affair with white men. Check out James Baldwin's books—that's what he's talking about.

Because Black men refuse to do in a concerted way what must be done to control white men. Since Black men are dying anyway I can't believe they are afraid of death. I think they don't want white men mad at them. I really do. And we watch white women really get into what they're all about with their liberation movement. The white woman's actions have been for an equality movement first of all and secondly have been patterned after Black men's. Only if she's asking for equality, the white man has given her everything by making her superior. She has the world at her feet, including, if you want to deal with it, all the Black men she wants; maybe not as much as they want but most certainly all she wants. And the only thing that has been denied her has been the Black woman. Check out a white woman going with a Black man and making a beeline to the first Black woman she spies to explain it. She didn't want the dude in the first place—she wants what stands behind him. If she's after my man she doesn't need to say anything to me at all; she got him. But white women and Black men are both niggers and both respond as such. He runs to the white man to explain his "rights" and she runs to us. And I think that's where they are both coming from. Probably any one of you knows a mixed couple—check it out. And the young white man doesn't know who he wants to be. He grows his hair long like his woman's; he dresses like our men and tries to run his home as Black women have.

We Black women are the single group in the West intact. And anybody can see we're pretty shaky. We are, however (all praises), the only group that derives its identity from itself. I think it's been rather unconscious but we measure ourselves by ourselves, and I think that's a practice we can ill afford to lose. For whatever combination of events that made us turn inward, We did. And we are watching the world trying to tear us apart. I don't think it will happen. I think the Lena Youngers will always survive and control in that happy sort of way they do. I don't really think it's bad to be used by someone you love. As Verta Mae pointed out, "What does it mean to walk five paces behind him?" If he needs it to know he's leading, then do it—or stop saying he isn't leading. Because it's clear that no one can outrun us. We Black women have obviously underestimated our strength. I used to think, why don't they just run ahead of us? But obviously we are moving pretty fast. The main thing we have to deal with is, What makes a woman? Once we decide that, everything else will fall into plan. As perhaps everything has. Black men have to decide what makes a man.

I'm sure it's easier for them to try to define us, which they frequently do in terms of white women because they frequently think of themselves in terms of white men. But if they ever would decide to define a Black man in Black terms I think they would have different expectations of us as women. I went to the opening of an African exhibit at the Brooklyn Museum and noticed only about a dozen Black men in a crowd of at least 200 people and I thought to myself, how odd—no Black men. Then I looked at the exhibit piece by piece and began to think I understood something. There was a beautiful door, from the Congo. And looking at that door I saw a man, a woman and several children in the yard and this cracker saying, "Your door is an excellent example of the Kishana people's art and I must take it back to Amsterdam." And this beautiful African, barefoot, with perhaps a single earring in his left ear, replies, "But this door is the door to my house and it is not for sale." And the woman, sensing something, stops the grinding of grain and begins gathering the children around her while the cracker goes on with "I must have the door. The museum needs it and I can make 50 dinars on it." And the African rises to his full height on his long, lithe legs, tribal markings dancing slightly on his face, eyes clear and hard, saying, "My family needs the door. It is mine. My father left it to me, as did his father to him. You may not have it. It is not for sale." And the cracker turns in rage to leave. Then two, perhaps three days later the missionary comes up saying, "My son, your door is needed in a great country far away from here. You will be blessed by our Heavenly Father if you will give your door to the merchant."

And this magnificent African, stooping by his doorway, playing with one of his children, shakes his head. "I would be cursed by my ancestors. Go now. Go away and leave us in peace." Then in the night the soldiers come with guns; the African responds with a spear. The fire ack-ack-acks from the barrels, the woman screams, the children scatter asking what is the matter, the man is stretched out in a pool of dark, murky liquid and the door is taken down, hoisted upon the shoulders of the Black mercenaries ("Don't know why Ododo wouldn't sell that door . . . could have made another"), walked to the sea and freighted back to Amsterdam so that it can be borrowed by the United States to show how the Kishana people lived in 1582.

And I began to understand why so few Black men had come, because it was not a door at all but dead ancestors murdered in their homes that they would see. Not a statue from Nigeria but a raped woman, a slit throat, a burned village. And even as I saw that I knew I would never really understand the reality of being a Black man. Men grow beards to protect the throat, have hair on their chest to protect the heart, have Afros to cushion the head blows; and these things become aesthetically acceptable, if not preferable, but they always have groundings in survival. My man and I can walk down the street together and if some other guy says something out of the way, it's an insult to me, it could be his life. I can walk away from words and gestures and still be a woman; he cannot and still be a man. So little of a Black man's existence relies on his acts. His women—mother, sisters, lovers—control his life and generally so irresponsibly that it can be frightening . . . it has frightened me to realize it. And sometimes Black women aren't very nice—for a lot of reasons; and sometimes we use our "power" against him—for a lot of reasons. I think some of the hostility is real and must be related to as such. We're angry and so are they but it's only when we admit it that we can get anywhere. All the poems dedicated to our brothers and the poems to our sisters are good but we should take the time to say to each other what we think we need, and we should do that honestly. I don't think a woman cares where she walks if you'll let her walk with you. And I don't think a man cares that she talks if she'll talk to him. And if we really understand we are born men and women and it's our choice whether or not we stay that way, I think a lot will change. But no one likes to admit, "Yes. I'm really put out with you." So the hidden hostility remains. And we cannot afford that. I don't think we can. I think we can do better. If now isn't a good time for the truth I don't see when we'll get to it.

Because I don't want my son to be a warrior. Or to go to some school where some insensitive bitch asks him why I'm not married, or where some cracker thinks he can run my son down anytime any kind of way he pleases. I read George Jackson's letters and I don't want my son to be a George or a Jonathan Jackson. Everything George has touched has turned sour. Everyone he has loved is now dead or dying. And this man must find a reason to live each and every day. We need some happiness in our lives. Some hope. Some love. No, I don't want anyone to be George Jackson. That much feeling bottled in a cell, in a prison, in California, in the United States. Something more definite must be settled. I didn't have a baby to see him be cannon fodder. I am cannon fodder. Something more definite must be decided. If it's a real war then he must be brave and true. If it's a mental war he must be Black and proud. But if it's a wake-the-people-up war Martin Luther King did it. Malcolm X did it. Stokely Carmichael did it. Rap Brown did it. And if the people aren't awake then perhaps the dreams are too good to be disturbed again. Perhaps Black people don't want Revolution at all. That too must be considered. I used to think the world needs what I need. But perhaps it doesn't. Because if it did we would relate to things like John and Robert Kennedy's assassinations. Those weren't individual acts that murdered them. All white people need to be taken out of power but they all clearly are not evil. If we were real we would relate to Angela Davis and forget the Commie hype. Most of the American Communist Party is FBI anyway. Didn't you read or watch *I Led Three Lives?* We would see Jimi Hendricks' and Janis Joplin's deaths as part of the same thing. And we could dig where Renault Robinson is coming from. Because we all know nobody sells what ain't being bought.

And I decided to be a writer because people said I was a genius and then would ask what I would become. And I couldn't see anywhere to go intellectually and thought I'd take a chance on feeling. I didn't want to get married, buy a five-room house in Madisonville and have lunch at Caproni's as my big event of the month. I could see becoming a bored, alcoholic social worker with a couple of kids I didn't want by a man I barely spoke to. And wondering at thirty-five what I'd done with my life. The second greatest thing that happened to me was getting kicked out of Fisk because I had to deal with my life. I could go back, join Delta (as all the other women in my family did), marry a Meharry man and go quietly insane; or I could go on to live. After knocking around and sponging off my parents for a while I went back to Fisk as a woman—not a little girl just being good like everybody said.

And I owe whatever mental health I possess to the care and devotion of my patient family and three mother surrogates—the Black nun I adopted, Theresa Elliott and Blanche Cowan. My father, my grandmother and those mother figures kept saying, "Don't look back." And my emotional growth I consider to be almost the sole product of Barbara Crosby. That's why I almost became a social worker. I wanted to do for someone what they have done for me. But I couldn't take graduate school when I realized the minute you institutionalize a problem you don't intend to solve it. Of course my grandmother did not live to see any of it. She had told me when I reentered Fisk she was just living to see me graduate. I, being young and not taking any of it to heart, graduated in February 1967 and she died in March. She was really a gas. She was the first to say and make me understand, You're mine, and I'll stick by you no matter what. Or to quote her accurately, "Let me know what you're doing and I'll stand between you and the niggers." And sometimes I look at my son, her second great-grandchild, and wonder what she would say about me. And sometimes I dream about coming into her home and her having practically a list of questions for me—"What is this abstinence they talk about for controlling birth?" or "Have you learned the flowers yet? Lord, I do so want you to be a lady!" And all the other little changes grandmothers carry you through. And I think I wanted to be famous because my mother deserves to make the world notice her existence. And my family has worked too hard to be ignored. I don't think I would have much cared if it weren't for them. But they deserve more. Other people put a lot of time and energy into me and they too deserve something.

And I understood that words have an innate reality, like noon is always noon, front or back, twelve o'clock or midnight, and *live* spelled backwards is *evil*, which white folks say we are, or *genesis* equals *gene*, which is the beginning. And love means nothing unless we are willing to be responsible for those who love us as well as those whom we love. That's one reason I am always cautious in personal relationships, because people don't just love you out of the blue—you let them. And people have loved me when I needed to be loved so as an adult I must give that love back to those who want it, or it all will have been for nothing. I think I am no different from any other colored girl who has to grow up and make and live by decisions. I think we are all capable of tremendous beauty once we decide we are beautiful or of giving a lot of love once we understand love is possible, and of making the world over in that image should we choose to. I really like to think a Black, beautiful, loving world is possible. I really do, I think.

FOR THE BEST IN PAPERBACKS, LOOK FOR THE

In every corner of the world, on every subject under the sun, Penguin represents quality and variety—the very best in publishing today.

For complete information about books available from Penguin—including Puffins, Penguin Classics, and Arkana—and how to order them, write to us at the appropriate address below. Please note that for copyright reasons the selection of books varies from country to country.

In the United Kingdom: Please write to *Dept. JC, Penguin Books Ltd, FREEPOST, West Drayton, Middlesex UB7 0BR.*

If you have any difficulty in obtaining a title, please send your order with the correct money, plus ten percent for postage and packaging, to *P.O. Box No. 11, West Drayton, Middlesex UB7 0BR*

In the United States: Please write to *Consumer Sales, Penguin USA, P.O. Box 999, Dept. 17109, Bergenfield, New Jersey 07621-0120.* VISA and MasterCard holders call 1-800-253-6476 to order all Penguin titles

In Canada: Please write to *Penguin Books Canada Ltd, 10 Alcorn Avenue, Suite 300, Toronto, Ontario M4V 3B2*

In Australia: Please write to *Penguin Books Australia Ltd, P.O. Box 257, Ringwood, Victoria 3134*

In New Zealand: Please write to *Penguin Books (NZ) Ltd, Private Bag 102902, North Shore Mail Centre, Auckland 10*

In India: Please write to *Penguin Books India Pvt Ltd, 706 Eros Apartments, 56 Nehru Place, New Delhi 110 019*

In the Netherlands: Please write to *Penguin Books Netherlands bv, Postbus 3507, NL-1001 AH Amsterdam*

In Germany: Please write to *Penguin Books Deutschland GmbH, Metzlerstrasse 26, 60594 Frankfurt am Main*

In Spain: Please write to *Penguin Books S. A., Bravo Murillo 19, 1° B, 28015 Madrid*

In Italy: Please write to *Penguin Italia s.r.l., Via Felice Casati 20, I-20124 Milano*

In France: Please write to *Penguin France S. A., 17 rue Lejeune, F–31000 Toulouse*

In Japan: Please write to *Penguin Books Japan, Ishikiribashi Building, 2–5–4, Suido, Bunkyo-ku, Tokyo 112*

In Greece: Please write to *Penguin Hellas Ltd, Dimocritou 3, GR–106 71 Athens*

In South Africa: Please write to *Longman Penguin Southern Africa (Pty) Ltd, Private Bag X08, Bertsham 2013*